Broken Sky

Part Six

Chris Wooding

Cover and illustrations by Steve Kyte

SCHOLASTIC

Other books by Chris Wooding:

Crashing

Point Horror Unleashed: Catchman

Kerosene

Endgame

Scholastic Children's Books,
Commonwealth House, 1-19 New Oxford Street,
London WC1A 1NU, UK
a division of Scholastic Ltd
London ~ New York ~ Toronto ~ Sydney ~ Auckland
Mexico City ~ New Delhi ~ Hong Kong

First published in the UK by Scholastic Ltd, 2000

Text copyright © Chris Wooding, 2000
Illustrations copyright © Steve Kyte, 2000

ISBN 0 439 01492 1

Typeset by M Rules
Printed by Bath Press, England

10 9 8 7 6 5 4 3 2 1

Check out the

Broken Sky

website

www.homestead.com/gar_jenna

Broken Sky

KERIAG QUEEN

FANE
ARACQ
GUARD

SNAGGLEBACKS

1

Flesh and Bone and Blood

"Hochi!" Peliqua cried as she shoved open what remained of the door to his hut.

Her arrival was greeted by a shriek from Elani, and accompanied by the sound of Hochi's hammer smashing into one of the Snappers that had been unwise enough to look around as she came through the door, breaking its bones like twigs. Fast as an eyeblink, Peliqua pulled free the weighted chain at her waist and sent it snaking out towards one of the two remaining creatures that had the big man and the Resonant backed into a corner.

It curled around the spindly wrist of one, arresting its arm in mid-strike; she pulled hard, yanking it off-balance and dragging it away from the couple, leaving Hochi to concentrate on the remaining attacker. As it stumbled towards her, she lashed the other end of the chain across the creature's face, smashing its jaw with a brutal crack and bringing a well of blood spewing from its mouth. Stunned, it was not fast enough to react as she ran one foot up on a stool and flipped over it, bringing the chain of her manriki-gusari looping around its neck. As she landed, she spun and pulled the chain taut, breaking the Snapper's neck over her shoulder, then flicked her weapon free and went to help Hochi.

The big man scarcely needed it. Heartened by the arrival of his companion, he had begun hefting his great warhammer in wide arcs, switching from a defensive stance to one of aggression. The Snapper was fast, but it was fighting in a confined space and there was nowhere to dodge the heavy swings. At the same time as Peliqua finished off her opponent, Hochi's adversary finally ran out of luck and was caught square in the chest, sending its spindly, broken body crashing against the wall of the hut, where it lay still.

"Mauni's Eyes, Peliqua, you know when to

make an entrance," Hochi said, crouching to hug the frightened Elani in one beefy arm.

"Really? You know I wanted to be in the theatre once, 'cause my mother said that to me and *she* thought I had talent, but of course we didn't have theatres any more 'cause of Macaan so I guess I . . . um. . ." she trailed off as she realized, by Hochi's expression, that this really wasn't the time. "Where's Jaan?" she said, trying a new tack.

"I don't know," he said. "I gave him and Iriqi the message from the Council, and they said they'd follow along later."

Elani looked at Peliqua with wide, teary eyes. "Do you think they're still *out* there?" she whispered, but Hochi cut in before the Kirin girl could reply.

"I'm sure they got in. They were up at the back gate of Base Usido, on the cliffs past the defences. That's where they'll be, I imagine. They'd have got inside when the alarm was raised."

"Okay, I'm gonna go see," she said, then suddenly shifted from an expression of dire concern to a cheery beam. "Holler if you need any more help."

"I'm gonna get Elani somewhere safe," Hochi said grimly. "You take care, okay?"

"You too. See ya, Elani."

Elani waved a goodbye, and then Peliqua darted back through the ruined doorway and into the camp again.

Outside, it was chaos. Somewhere beyond the perimeter wall, the giant beetle-like mukhili had been released from their caves and were rampaging through the ranks of the enemy, guided by desert-folk in howdahs. The mukhili had been invaluable during the battle at the Ley Warren during the Integration; coming from the southern deserts of the Dominions, they were massive mobile fortresses that the people of the region had learned to harness for war. Transported with the rest of the army after the Ley Warren exploded, they were kept in the caves that honeycombed the base of the cliffs; but now they had been brought into the battle, and were sowing havoc.

Inside the walls, it was even more hectic. Banes swirled between the leaping Snappers and the hulking Snagglebacks as they fought with the

Parakkans. A cohort of riders, on pakpaks and horses both, had raided the stables for mounts and come out fighting, using both weapons and spirit-stones in an attempt to drive away the Rift-beasts from the living-quarters.

Everywhere there were little islands of conflict; a woman locked in single combat with a Snaggleback twice her weight; a group of Kirin children of about Gerdi's age that leaped and scampered among the roofs of the huts, shooting poison-tipped arrows at the creatures that ran below them; a cluster of Banes feeding on what was left after a group of Dominion-folk had been cornered and killed by some Snappers. But Peliqua could not stop to help without entangling herself in the constant combat, and she had other concerns. Where was her brother?

She was forced to stop and fight twice before she reached the foot of the wide, flat section of cliff that Base Usido backed up against. It was as she had suspected; while all the lifts outside the Base had been lowered to the plain floor to prevent any of the creatures somehow using the mechanisms to get down the cliff wall, all the lifts within the perimeter had been *raised* the moment that they got word of the breach, to stop the reverse happening. They had taken as many of the children that they could, along with anyone else who was incapable of fighting, and brought them to the sanctuary of high ground, where they would hopefully be safe behind the clifftop defences. Peliqua didn't doubt that any creature who tried scaling the cliffs would get an unfriendly reception at the top.

Looking around to be sure that none of the creatures were near by, she darted into a small hut of weathered iron that stood next to the huge cogs and pulleys set into the stone of the cliffs. Inside, among the several layers of Machinist instrumentation that ran around the small room at waist-and-eye height, there was a small speaker grille. She pressed the button next to it and put her mouth close.

"This is Peliqua. Is anyone up there?"

There was no reply.

"Is anyone—" she began, but she was cut off as another voice came through, crackly and faint, its nuances mangled by the crude technology that worked it.

"Peliqua, this is Bicio. We're holding out up here, but only just. We need reinforcements."

"Is my brother up there? Jaan? A halfbreed boy, probably with that great big Koth Taraan?"

"Listen, girl, I haven't seen them and I don't have time to go look for them. You want them, come up here and find them yourself."

"Send me a lift down," she replied. "The smallest one."

"You make sure it's only you that comes up," Bicio said sternly, and cut the connection.

Peliqua released the button and ran outside again. A Snapper scampered between two huts to her right, but it was intent on something else and did not see her. She double-checked in case anything was trying to sneak up on her, and then looked up at the cliff, where a narrow metal cage – big enough for two people at most – was clanking down towards her. She scanned around, and found a spot behind a hut where she could hide until it arrived; standing out in the open like she was, trouble was bound to find her. She watched the lift descend and settle with a grinding thump and a hiss of steam.

As she prepared to cross the open ground between her and the lift, she hoped that fortune would be with her. It wasn't. The moment she broke cover and ran, a Snaggleback that had been ambling across the blood-soaked grass near by sensed the movement, its nostrils flaring, and began to bound towards her, screeching its *yip! yip!* cry.

She saw it coming out of the corner of her eye as she scrambled into the cage, yanking the lever upwards to start its ascent as she shut the door behind her with her other hand. For one terrible moment, the cage didn't move; then the mechanism kicked in, and it started to climb. She pressed her back to the cliff side of the cage and held her breath, watching the Snaggleback charge towards her. It had a lot of ground to cover, but the lift was slow, too cursed *slow*! As it neared, her transfixed eyes skittered over its thick, taut bunches of muscle, its protruding jaws, and the forest of stiff, spiny hairs on its back that gave its species their nickname. Snappers she could handle, but one of these? And on her own? She doubted it.

Go faster! she urged the unheeding metal, as it lifted her higher. But would it be high enough?

The Snaggleback pounded over the grass, becoming gradually smaller beneath her. She must be thirty feet up by now, at least. Surely well out of its reach?

Wrong again. It took one long stride and then launched itself upwards and towards her, its grotesque jaws wide, its cheeks and lips skinned back across its skull. Peliqua cried out in fear and shock as it crashed into the cage, making it shudder and almost ripping it from its moorings and sending them both plummeting. It tried to get a handhold, failed, and slid off the dented metal bars, falling away; but then one strong hand shot out, grabbing the bottom of the cage just by Peliqua's booted feet, its fingers punching through the mesh. The lift shuddered and groaned, unable to take the immense weight of the beast.

But then a second Snaggleback appeared, attracted by the struggle, racing across the ground and leaping up for the cage. Peliqua screamed;

but right at that moment, the mechanism of the lift lurched and pulled her upward a few feet. The Snaggleback fell short, grabbing on to its hanging companion. The lift screeched, beginning to pull free of its securing-bolts; but the mesh in the floor gave way first. The Snaggleback's tenuous hold was suddenly foiled as the metal under its fingertips bent downwards, unable to support the weight of two creatures. With a shrieking *yip!* it fell free, its companion with it, and the two of them smashed into the rocky ground at the base of the cliffs and remained there.

Peliqua breathed an oath in relief as the cage began to ascend again, arranging herself so that she was not standing near the hole in the floor. The lift limped up the cliff face, carrying her to the top, and when she got out she had never been so glad to feel solid earth beneath her feet.

On the cliff top, things were only a little better than down below.

When Base Usido had first been constructed, it had been necessary to build it up against the cliffs that surrounded the huge, sunken plain because they had not had enough materials to build an encircling wall for the whole base. Building against the cliffs meant they did not have to worry about being attacked from behind, and they could concentrate on defending one area from the Rift-beasts that roamed the plains while they erected a semicircular perimeter wall. However, as time went on and more resources became available, it became obvious that this had been a mistake. There were many creatures that could scale down the cliffs at Base Usido's back easily, and they could get inside the walls that way.

So it was decided that the top of the cliffs would be guarded, too, in an attempt to prevent this happening. Lifts were built to haul materials up and down the cliff face. The forest of haaka and wychwood was cut back, and another semicircular wall was constructed, forming a small island of safety at the top of the cliffs where weapons and stores were stockpiled. It was there to guard Base Usido's back; but as Peliqua stepped out of the lift, she saw that it was only barely managing to do that.

The hordes were battering at the walls,

oblivious to the force-cannon blasts that ripped into them from the turret-mounted weapons. Their dead had blunted the spikes, sheathing their edges in flesh and bone and blood, and now the Parakkans fought like demons to keep the creatures from clambering over and into the compound. The air was dense with screeches, cries, and the repetitive *whumph* of force-bolts. All around them, the Banes swirled madly, curling among the carnage and feeding on the dead, writhing away if anyone came near. She spotted Calica in the thick of it, and made her way towards the wall, through the clusters of frightened children and the elderly that sheltered here. It was safer for them here than below, where the creatures had already broken through and were rampaging across the Base.

Climbing up the iron rungs of a ladder, she hurried along the narrow ledge where the defenders lashed and sliced to keep the creatures down. Calica was hacking wildly with her katana, her face and chest and arms sprayed in blood and dirt, streaked through with sweat. She looked exhausted, and her usual precision and skill with her weapon had been abandoned through tiredness for clumsy strikes.

"Calica!" Peliqua said. "Take a break!" She stepped in to cover for her, and Calica gratefully took a step back, panting, while the Kirin girl brought her manriki-gusari to bear on the invaders, dislodging handholds, smashing into foreheads, entangling and killing.

"Where's Jaan?" Calica shouted over the noise, when she had taken a few breaths.

"Isn't he here?" Peliqua shouted back, not taking her eyes from the battle.

"Haven't seen him. Or the Koth Taraan."

"You think they're still out there?"

"If they are, they'll be safe enough. Banes don't go for anything without a spirit-stone."

"They went for that little boy, Paani," Peliqua argued.

Calica hesitated. "They were out by the caves. Maybe they'll be okay."

Peliqua felt a terrible helplessness overwhelm her. Maybe? *Maybe* they'll be okay? Maybe wasn't good enough. But if they were out there and she was in here, there was nothing she could do. She had always been there to look after him, to cajole him when he got down, to defend him when other children mocked his halfbreed features. Now he was alone, except for a creature that wasn't even human.

What chance did he have without her? she thought, and blinked back tears as she fought on.

Jaan pressed himself hard against the cold, dank stone and tried not to breathe, his yellow eyes fixed on the glowing white of the Bane as it slipped through the air further up the tunnel, its snakelike body curling in the still darkness, leaving tiny streamers of light behind it as it went. Its wide mouth opened and closed as it turned, as if it could taste Jaan's presence; but then it coiled upon itself and headed back up the tunnel, away from where they hid.

He stayed still for a long while, listening to the scuff and scrape of the Snappers and Snagglebacks that roamed the caves in search of him. The Snappers, like him, did not need more than a glimmer of light to see by, while the

Snagglebacks had no eyes at all; and they were hunting for him now, led here by a Bane.

*((**Your home is a dangerous place to live**))* Iriqi commented silently, the words tinged with an ironic blue.

"It's not like we had much of a choice," Jaan whispered back to the hulking form that stood next to him, sheltered from sight by an alcove in the rock. "And if that Bane hadn't seen us, we'd never have been in danger at all."

*((**Why?**))*

"They say the Banes only go for spirit-stones. They don't usually attack the living. It's the Snagglebacks and Snappers who—"

*((**But we don't have any spirit-stones**))* Iriqi interrupted.

"That's what puzzles me." He drew back into the alcove, and slid down the wall to the ground, dwarfed by the huge, armoured frame of his companion.

*((**It senses the Communion**))* the Koth Taraan stated.

Jaan looked up at it, the tiniest glimmer of illumination dancing across the planes of its eyes.

"And you're gonna tell me what that is, right?"

((The link that the Koth Taraan share. Each of us are connected to each other, but no link is stronger than with the Koth Macquai. It holds the Communion in its breast))

"That glowing light Kia mentioned?" he queried, remembering the few times that Kia had spoken on their way back from the Unclaimed Lands.

((It is passed on by each Koth Macquai on their death to their successor. It holds the memories of the deceased, and therefore the memories of all the Brethren. And they hold the memories of those that they succeeded, and so on. It has been so for thousands of generations. Our memory is eternal))

Jaan nodded to himself. At last he understood what Iriqi meant when he said that same phrase, back at the Koth Taraan's settlement. That was why the only way to entirely erase the Koth Taraan would be to kill them and destroy the Communion. That was why the younger Brethren feared Macaan, and wanted to help Parakka. In hiding, they had been trying to preserve their species and their culture. Now they wanted to do the same by attacking.

"You think the Bane's after you?"

((It senses something it has not sensed before. A power it does not recognize. It wants to feed))

"How do you *know* that?"

((I have many wiser Brethren to advise me))

Jaan shook his head, the tangled ropes of his hair clinking with the ornaments that were sewn there. He could never fully accept the fact that Iriqi shared a link with every other member of his species, and was in constant contact at all times. It was a human thing, to think of someone as an individual. As such, he tended to forget that everything he told the Koth Taraan was instantly relayed to each of his Brethren.

And he had talked to Iriqi about some deeply personal things during the time they had spent together; as one alien to another, they shared something of a rapport. When talking to a creature neither Dominion-born or Kirin, Jaan did not find himself being self-conscious about his halfbreed face. It was only by contrast that he realized how withdrawn he was with his other friends, how his silence was a product of his own shame. No matter how much he protested against it, and despite his sister's best efforts, he was ashamed to be a halfbreed. It had been drilled into him since he was born, through the taunts of the children in their hometown, through the looks of disgust on elder folk's faces as he passed. Even with a friend such as Gerdi, who harboured none of their prejudice, who had never heeded Aurin's propaganda; even with him, he felt inferior. He couldn't help it.

But not with Iriqi. Iriqi was too far removed from either race to provoke the shame that he always kept just beneath the surface. And Jaan liked that. It put him at ease; a state of mind that he had not been in for a very long time.

((We should go)) Iriqi said. *((The Rift-beasts are getting closer))*

Jaan listened, and realized that it was true. The snuffles and scratches from all around them were louder now, coming through the walls or echoing down the long, narrow tunnels.

"We should try and make our way round to the entrance," Jaan whispered. Then, as it suddenly occurred to him, he asked: "You remember the way?"

((Our memory is eternal)) the Koth Taraan said in a faint pink cloud of amusement.

"Yeah, that's what I thought," Jaan muttered, and they headed off through the tunnels.

The Koth Taraan were a surprisingly stealthy people, for all their huge size and cumbersome bulk. Despite the fact that Iriqi filled up the tunnel as he lumbered along, he made hardly any noise. Jaan supposed that, as a race, they were used to hiding – something that they shared with Parakka – but it still defied belief that a creature so heavy could have a tread so light.

They crept through the thick, underground darkness, surrounded by ghostly scratches and scrapes, which sounded frighteningly close at times and at others would be distant and barely audible. The rock twisted sound so that Jaan's ears were unreliable; and his eyes were scarcely better, for even with his Kirin low-light vision it was difficult to make out more than a vague impression of the shape of the tunnel they followed. He hoped that his pursuers were having the same problem, but he doubted it. What did darkness matter to creatures like the Banes, which produced their own light, or Snagglebacks, which had no eyes?

They had gone scarcely fifty metres when something moved across the lighter dark of a tunnel junction ahead, and paused suddenly. Jaan froze; by its size, it could only be a Snaggleback. Behind him, Iriqi became similarly motionless.

((If it comes for us, get behind me)) the Koth Taraan said silently in grave, iron-shod colours.

But there was really no question that it would. By whatever sense the Snagglebacks hunted, whether it was scent or vibration, hearing or something else, they were right in its path. Jaan felt his stomach sink as it turned its silhouetted head towards them, and its jaws slid out of the sheath of its lips; and then it loosed the distinctive cry of its race, sounding the alarm, that the prey had been found.

Jaan looked past Iriqi, down the tunnel the other way, but he already knew what he would see. It was a long and featureless tube of rock that they had travelled down, with no side-arteries in which to lose themselves, no escape route. And besides, there were already shapes moving at the far limit of his vision, galloping towards them.

"There's at least two coming up behind us," he said urgently. "You take them, Iriqi, and I'll –" he clashed his forearms together, and the long blades of his dagnas sprang out of their hollow wooden tubes, "– take this one."

((Agreed. Be careful)) A purple-blue wash of concern.

Jaan didn't reply, his eyes fixed on the Snaggleback as it crept towards them, not yet charging but slinking insidiously closer. Iriqi turned around, rotating with a quiet shuffling noise, and they stood back-to-back in the tunnel, the halfbreed boy and the Koth Taraan.

"Come on!" Jaan challenged, and the creature responded instantly, accelerating and pounding towards him on all fours. The others followed suit, tearing up the tunnel towards their prey.

The one that had spotted them reached the pair first, hurtling into them with suicidal abandon. Snagglebacks were not clever fighters; they relied on brute force to overwhelm their prey. But despite the closeness of the tunnel, Jaan still had space to jump out of the way as it approached, slashing down at it as it passed and slicing deeply into the rippling expanse of its ribs. Screeching a high *yip!*, it slammed into the armoured hide of Iriqi's back, scarcely even rocking the Koth Taraan. Jaan heard something break inside it, but he could not afford to wait and see if it had been finished off. He plunged his right dagna deep into the nape of its neck; it spasmed once, violently, and then went limp.

But its approach had masked another problem: there were two more shapes coming down Jaan's side of the corridor, two more that he hadn't seen. And there was the Bane, suddenly appearing from around the corner, curling and twisting as it followed them, casting its ethereal light.

The two on Jaan's side and the two approaching Iriqi converged at almost the same moment, a savage mass of fangs and nails. At least one of them was a Snapper, but Jaan could barely see, and he was too preoccupied with the cut and parry of survival to take the time to care. Somewhere behind him, he heard a nauseating crack as Iriqi smashed one of his opponents against the tunnel wall with his outsize claws. A late parry left him with shallow score-marks down his arm. He was vaguely aware of the Bane, hanging back, waiting to feed after its companions had finished off the prey. But they were finding Iriqi a harder opponent than they thought; for Jaan heard the shriek of a Snapper as it was crushed by the Koth Taraan's immense strength, even as he fought off the grasping claws of the Snaggleback, and. . .

Suddenly he was aware of a bright movement, and the Bane darted past him and wrapped around the narrow part of Iriqi's arm, between the huge shoulder plate and his massive forearm.

"Iriqi!" Jaan cried, but he could do nothing more. The Bane bit deep, its body dissipating as it flowed into the wound, entering the Koth Taraan's body, seizing its mind.

And then the darkness was pounded by a terrible screech, a noise such as Jaan had never heard before, which sanded his nerves and made his body shudder. Even his opponents paused and drew back, as the corridor was suddenly filled with a million tiny tadpoles of light, skittering away from the Koth Taraan's body and fading into nowhere. Jaan stood, uncertain, watching the huge creature as it turned around to face them. What had happened to it? Was it hurt? Would it –?

((Get behind me, human child)) it said again, and this time its words were soaked in black anger. Jaan did so, slipping around its huge leg; but the remaining Snapper and Snaggleback seemed less than eager to continue the fight now, and they turned and ran, disappearing up the corridor.

"What happened?" he asked in wonderment. "What happened to the Bane?"

((Later)) came the reply. *((Let us go back to Base Usido))*

"But it's—"

((I do not think the Base will be under attack for much longer))

The effect was instant and simultaneous. The defenders did not know what they were seeing, but the reaction of the besieging hordes told them it had to be good. All across the battlefield, even inside the walls of Base Usido where the invaders still ran amok, sparkling fountains of light suddenly burst forth, swirling upwards like the dust devils in the southern deserts of the Dominions, miniature tornadoes of luminescence that dissolved into hundreds upon thousands of tiny wriggles of light and then disappeared. The light seemed to be coming from the creatures themselves, the Snagglebacks and Snappers – only certain ones, perhaps one in twenty-five or more, but it was as if something had flowed out of their bodies. At the same time, the Banes that flitted across the battlefield lifted their voices as one in an unearthly screech and exploded in a shower of light.

And though none of the Parakkans knew what had happened, one thing was certain. The tide had turned. The enemy were beaten.

The assault was over.

From high in the sky over the Fin Jaarek mountain range, the Rifts were a dark, heavily forested smear, stretching for vast miles in a long strip between the feet of the mountains and the plains to the west. It was dangerous to fly over, because of the many wild wyverns and other airborne beasts that made the shattered lands their home. But the Princess Aurin had stepped up patrols recently, tripling their frequency and spreading them out over a wider area, and even the Rifts now were to be flown over whenever it was judged safe to do so. Not that there was much point; no Riders dared go low enough to see anything in the dim Kirin Taq light, and the trees obscured almost everything. It would only be possible to find something in the maze of the Rifts if they were skimming the treetops and flew directly over it, and that was hardly likely.

But there *was* a patrol that particular cycle, three Riders on wyvern-back, their red armour dull in the glow of the eclipsed sun, winging silently through the sky. They were skimming the edge of the Rifts, following the feet of the mountains around, making no more than a cursory check of the black expanse beneath them. They had not been told what to look for, for Aurin was keeping the news of Parakka's re-emergence as secret as she could to prevent word leaking back to her father; but they knew, by the sudden increase in patrols, that something was happening in Kirin Taq. Something big.

And it was only really a case of bad fortune for Parakka. The Riders happened to be flying through that still night sky when the eruption of light from the dissipating Banes lit up a small section of the forest beneath them like a flare. One pointed, and they wheeled around, watching the blazing white, memorizing its position before diving down towards it. It had faded before they reached it.

They did not see the sudden change in the battle. Nor did they see the Snagglebacks and Snappers routed, turning and fleeing back into the forests or panicking on the plains where they were crushed by the enormous mukhili. They did not see the Parakkans turning their attention inward to purge the invaders that had got inside the wall. But they heard the erratic *whumph* of the force-cannons, and they heard the shrieking of the wyverns as they mopped up the last of the enemy that could not escape, and so they passed silently overhead and turned their mounts towards Fane Aracq, where the Princess would be very interested to hear their news. . .

2

A Sign of Weakness

Corm strode through the bone-smooth corridors of Fane Aracq, his mechanical eyes clicking and chattering as they peered out from above the rim of his high, stiff collar. His black greatcoat flapped around his feet as he walked, his face set hard. It was time for their regular three-cycle report to the Princess. Usually, it was a routine, even a pleasure. Today, he did not know how he was going to handle it.

The prisoner had been allowed out. He was permitted to exercise in the courtyard, under escort. He was permitted to practise with weapons, albeit with a heavy guard. These were not the sort of privileges extended to a prisoner who was soon to be executed.

He hoped he had himself under control, but he

was not confident that the outrage he felt at the Princess's actions would not leak into his voice and manner when he spoke to her. What next? Would she remove his Damper Collar? Would she give him the run of the palace? What did Aurin think she was *doing*?

Up here, nearer the Princess's chambers, the smokeless wychwood torches had been replaced by white glowstones in the corridors. It was a gesture of excessive opulence, for the white stones were rare and much-prized because their light showed colours true, instead of the orange hue from common glowstones. Corm barely noticed the change as he walked, his mind fixed only on what he must say and how he had to say it. Minutes later, he arrived at Aurin's chambers.

Tatterdemalion was already there, crouching by the massive wall-mirror, a scrawny, misshapen mass of rags, belts and metal. Aurin, by contrast, looked a picture of perfection, sleek and elegant as she stood in wait for Corm's arrival. He entered with as much composure as he could, bowed and then awaited her command.

"Greetings once again to you both," she said.

"What developments in my realm?" The question was asked with the barest minimum of interest, even less than she usually mustered. She seemed preoccupied. After a moment, she looked up at the Machinist. "Corm?"

"Things are as ever, my Princess. I have nothing to report. But I do have a question, if I may."

"Is it about the prisoner?" she asked sharply.

"Yes," he replied.

"Then guard your tongue carefully this time, Corm," she warned. "What is it?"

Corm hesitated before speaking, wondering if it was entirely wise to risk her wrath when today it seemed so easily aroused. "I have been informed that the prisoner has been allowed certain extra privileges, my Princess. . ." he began.

"We've been over this ground, yes?" she interrupted. "I have told you the reason behind my generosity to him."

She *was* touchy. "I am not presuming to question your plan, my Princess," Corm said hastily. "I merely wish to know if you still intend to execute the prisoner after the location of the Parakkan base is revealed."

"Of course," she said. "What *else* would I do with him? Set him free?" She paused, thinking. "Perhaps I would keep him for a short while, the better to use him to understand the minds of my enemy. But there will come a time when his usefulness expires, yes?"

"I understand, my Princess."

"And what of the stirrings in the Machinist Citadel?" she asked, changing the subject.

"No change," he replied. "Your father keeps trade up with the Guild, and until he ceases to do so things are unlikely to shift drastically."

"Tatterdemalion?" she prompted, turning to the silent creature.

+++ The Jachyra are loyal to you +++

"And do *you* have anything to report?" she asked, turning away and pacing across the room, her thigh-high white boots clicking on the creamstone floor as they moved beneath her long dress.

+++ A minor incident in Taitai, my lady. Two members of the ruling council were found to be sympathizers with the recent uprising in Kitika. They disapproved of your methods of crushing

the rebellion. **We have watched them for a time. Last cycle they began making treasonous statements to the villagers in the support of Parakka. We took them; we await your decision on their fate +++** The Jachyra's report faded off into a static hum, and his telescopic eye whirred, adjusting focus, as he watched the Princess.

She did not reply with her usual speed. In fact, she spent a long minute in silence, looking out of one of the wind-holes at the velvety-blue sky.

"Princess? Are you alright?" Corm asked. She jumped infinitesimally in surprise, suddenly realizing where she was again.

"I'm sorry. What?" she said, turning around and leaning against the sill, her long index and middle finger resting in the bridge of her small nose in thought.

+++ The sympathizers in Taitai +++ Tatterdemalion said, then added: **+++ They *are* Councillors, my lady +++**

"Do they have families?" she asked.

+++ They do +++ came the crackling reply. **+++ Shall we execute them also? +++**

Aurin looked up, and a tired shadow seemed

to cross her pretty features. "Scourge them, yes? Just the Councillors, not their families. Ten times each, in the public square of Taitai. Make sure everyone knows why, and that everyone is clear that a repeat occurrence will result in the village being burnt to the ground. With everyone inside."

"Princess!" Corm exclaimed, before his better judgement could stop him.

"You have a better suggestion?" Aurin said quietly, unmistakable menace in her voice.

"It's just . . . Parakkan sympathizers are always punished by death. At *least*," the Machinist said. "Their families almost always suffer with them, to discourage traitors. It has worked so far, Princess. If we become lax, people will see it as a sign of weakness and—"

"I don't care," she interrupted. "I am heartsick of killing. And the policy of execution *hasn't* worked so far, Corm, because we still have to do it. I am not suggesting we change; but for this particular instance, I choose to have mercy on them. I will not hear any argument. And if you *dare* suggest that this is the prisoner's doing, I will have you scourged with them."

Corm bowed his head and was silent, but he seethed inside. The very fact that she had been thinking of his next comment proved to him that he was right.

"Unless there is anything else, you may go. Both of you," she said, her tone ending the audience more finally than her words did. They both made parting gestures of respect and left.

When she was alone again, she sat down on a cushioned bench of creamstone, moulded out of the wall, and poured herself a glass of Dominion summerleaf wine. She swirled it thoughtfully as she looked at herself in the huge mirror that seemed to grow seamlessly out of the wall. She knew what Corm thought; it was written plainly on his half-Augmented face, despite his attempts to hide it. What rankled was that he was right, and she knew it. It *was* Ryushi that was affecting her this way. Over the span of their visits, he had urged her to think of the people that she ruled over, to put herself in their place, to empathize with them; and gradually, unstoppably, it had begun to seep through.

She felt guilty. She felt guilty, because she had

begun to imagine the sinking feeling, the terrible cold that the traitors in Kitika must have felt as her pronouncement of death was passed on to them, the horror as they were told that their families would be sent into slavery in the mines for generations to come. It made her sad, but it also made her ashamed. It was she that had done that to them, and even though they were just lowly villagers, their emotions, their *humanity* was no less than hers.

She had never thought about it before. Never. And now she was being forced to. Because try as she might, she could not seem to stay away from the Dominion boy in her prison; and while she kept on visiting him, under the paper-thin pretence of extracting information, he kept on making her think about it. And now she couldn't stop.

What was *wrong* with her?

She got up, leaving the untouched glass of wine, and walked through the corridors of her palace, taking a route that had recently become well-known to her. On the way, she ignored the small bows of fealty that the Guardsmen and retainers made, and avoided any of the nobles who might want to take up her time with idle talk. She headed for the cells, and when she got there, she dismissed the Guardsman on watch and told him to wait further up the corridor.

Slipping the key in the lock, she opened the cell door and stepped inside.

Ryushi looked up from the bench as she entered, raising his face from the pillow where it had rested a moment before. He blinked blearily at her, his short, thick tentacles of blond hair falling about his elfin face, then smiled a greeting and raised his tired body into a sitting position.

"I woke you? I'm sorry," she said.

"S'okay," Ryushi replied, rubbing one eye with the heel of his palm. "The exercise yard pretty much burned me out. Been cooped up so long I was getting out of shape, and I pushed myself a little hard." He let his hands fall to his lap and looked at her. "I have you to thank for that?" he asked, though he already knew the answer.

She smiled an affirmative, standing where she was.

"You want to sit down?" he offered, indicating

the bench next to him. It seemed absurd, that he should be offering the hospitality of his prison cell to the one who put him there; but she declined anyway.

"I won't stay long," she said. "You're tired?"

Ryushi's eyelids were already drooping. He nodded wearily.

"I just came to tell you," she said. "Tatterdemalion found some defectors in Taitai. I . . . spared them."

His face came suddenly alive, momentarily seeming to shed the drowsiness that fogged it. "You did? That's . . . that's great."

She was a little taken aback. She had expected a sarcastic comment, some sort of snide remark about how she was *so* generous to let them live when it was her that was choking their freedom of choice in the first place. Instead, he seemed genuine, if a little surprised.

"Well . . . I just came to tell you, that's all," she said, suddenly awkward. This was no way for a Princess to act, she told herself; but at the same time, she felt strangely good about it, childishly happy. "I'll go now, yes?"

"You could stay if you wanted. I'm not tired," Ryushi said, his eyes beginning to droop again.

She laughed lightly. "Go to sleep. I will see you again soon." She went to let herself out, hearing him nestle back on to the sleeping-bench behind her. Opening the ivory cell door, she almost walked into Corm, who peered at her with his Augmented eyes, his face half-covered by his collar.

"What is it, Corm?" she snapped, surprise making her short-tempered.

"I have just received word, Princess. Three Riders have come in with some very interesting information. You should hear it."

She frowned, disappointed that her elation had been soured by Corm's disapproval before she had a chance to savour it. "Very well. I will see them in the audience chamber. Go and bring them there."

Corm bowed, a slight movement of his bald head, and then stalked away past the waiting Guardsman sentry. Aurin stood where she was for a moment, the cell door still ajar next to her. On impulse, she looked back through the oval spy-holes, and saw Ryushi lying on his side, his ribs rising and falling with the slow breath of sleep. For a moment, she didn't move. Then she pushed the door open, very quietly, her heart beginning to flutter in her chest. Ryushi did not stir.

Softly, she took two quick steps towards him and gently leaned down to kiss the lobe of his ear. It was a fleeting touch, the soft pressure and moistness of her lips; and then she left in haste, closing the door behind her and locking it.

Ryushi lay listening to her footsteps recede for a long time before he opened his eyes.

Gerdi slept. Curled up like a foetus in a thin, threadbare woollen blanket, he was oblivious to the twenty-foot drop that waited a few inches away from the curve of his spine. He was not aware of the dim light that barely touched him from the single orange glowstone in the room, obscured behind a bookcase; nor of the slightly dry and musty odour of the old library. He was exhausted, stone-drained. He had to sleep, and sleep he did.

The library was ideal. Its poor lighting and the stiffness of the door betrayed how little it was used, and the tall bookcases that rose high above him provided perfect hiding places. He had scaled one that was pushed up against the wall, furthest from the light, and clambered on top of it. On the thick ledge of wood he had wearily made his bed. Even if someone came looking, the stepladder in the corner was only high enough so that a tall man could barely reach the top shelf. Someone could take a book from right under Gerdi and not see him.

He was safe, or as safe as he could be in the heart of Fane Aracq.

Five cycles now he had spent in the halls of Aurin's palace. Five cycles of constant watchfulness, alertness, fear. It wore him down. His nerves were shredded. His mind was clogged with remembering different mannerisms, faces and speech patterns, and who to use on which people. But now, finally, he was nearing his goal. He knew at last where they were keeping Ryushi.

The last few cycles had all followed a similar pattern. Keeping to sparsely-walked areas of the palace, he would use whatever guise he had adopted to get into conversation with somebody else of a higher rank than he, and then make his way further into the palace. The chaotic exterior betrayed an ingeniously planned system of corridors where certain areas and sections could be restricted simply by putting a few Guards on a few entrances. A whole slice of the palace would be for visiting nobility only, and the encircling corridors for their retainers; while another cluster of rooms might be for highborn ladies, and no men allowed. It was a labyrinth of sections within sections within sections, and at the heart of it, he imagined, would be the Princess's chambers. Thankfully, the password system did not operate inside the main section of the palace. He was able to pass by the checks by adopting the faces of those people with authorization, after studying them for a while beforehand to get the nuances of their actions right. It was all done so as not to arouse suspicion, and so far he had succeeded. There had been tricky situations when he had almost walked into the real-life person he was impersonating, and one interesting conversation with an ex-lover of another.

But it would all be for nothing if Jutar came back early from leave and anyone asked him about his head wound.

Then, finally, he had hit pay dirt. A sentry who recognized the Guard Captain he was impersonating hailed him as he was looking for a new victim to copy.

"Going to the prison section, Mujio?"

Gerdi had halted, frowning. The corridor had been only a random choice, but now he pointed down it, and said with the exaggerated sarcasm that was Mujio's mode of speech: "You mean the prisons are down here? I've had so little cause to visit them, I'd never have guessed."

The sentry laughed at his jest, but he'd confirmed the underlying question. The prison section was indeed down that way, and he went far enough along the smooth, white corridor to confirm that before doubling back and finding the library where he now slept. It was important to be at full strength when he went to rescue Ryushi. If Ryushi was still there at all, he reminded himself.

3

Simply a Circle

When she came back to him, perhaps a half-cycle later, he was awake again. He had thought that he would never drop off, so turbulent was his mind after the Princess's last visit; but the wolves of sleep had stalked him stealthily, and they were too great in number to avoid for long. Even his sleep was no refuge, though; his dreams continued to sort and shuffle through the dilemmas that had been presented to him, visiting him with visions and possibilities until he was no longer sure what had happened and what hadn't.

The Princess had *kissed* him. All this time, he had been wondering what she had up her sleeve, what she was doing, why she spent hours talking with him about nothing. He had thought it might be a trick at first, but that had been only the most likely of many possible reasons. He had even thought that she might be lonely, that she talked to him because he was the only one who did not treat her like a Princess, or pussyfoot around her in fear of her wrath; but he had dismissed that as ridiculous. She was the enemy, the daughter of Macaan, strong-willed and stubborn, and not prone to those kind of weaknesses.

But this . . . the idea that she might be in *love* with him had never crossed his mind until now.

It wasn't his fault. After all, he had spent much of his childhood under their father's strict training regime, and most of his time on the Stud had been spent with his twin. While there were many boys tending the wyverns, there were only few girls, and none of them could really measure up to the lighthearted tomboyishness of Kia. Then, of course, when Osaka Stud was destroyed, he had been forced to devote himself to Parakka, and had no time for any other, more frivolous interests. Naïvety had been pretty much his defining characteristic for a long time, and the ways of the opposite sex were no exception.

The enemy, the daughter of the one who had been partly responsible for the murder of his family, was falling in love with Ryushi. And the hornet's nest of confusion it had stirred up within him was not something that could easily be quieted.

His chest was taut with anticipation as he heard the key turn in the lock, and when she stepped through, it was as if he saw her for the first time. Her long, slender neck; the delicate curve of her collarbone; the gentle slope of her nose; her narrow, dark eyes. His breathing shallowed out as she came in, and he stared at her; and she, as if sensing the change, paused for a moment.

"Are you alright?" she said, and the spell was dislodged enough for Ryushi to speak.

"I'm okay," he replied, from where he sat on the edge of his bench. It was then that he noticed the air of sadness around the Princess, a sorrowful quality to her expression. "Are you?"

"Of course," she answered dismissively, closing the door behind her. "Why wouldn't I be?"

"You tell me."

She turned back to him, a sudden archness in her voice. "Nothing is wrong."

He shrugged. "Okay then. Will you sit?"

"No," she said distractedly. "No, I think not."

She stood there, looking around the bare creamstone walls of the cell. It was obvious she had something to say, but did not know how to say it. It was —

"Your necklace," Ryushi heard himself begin, interrupting even his own thoughts. "You wear many different clothes, but they're always matched to your necklace, and I've never seen you without it. Why is that, Aurin?"

He had wondered about it for some time, but he had never asked the question until now. He had not intended to put it so directly. It just came out to fill the awkward void in the conversation. But so preoccupied was he with wondering where the question had come from, that he did not notice the sudden softening of Aurin's features, the almost visible melting inside her. Without realizing it, he had called her by her name instead of her title for the first time.

She broke into a little smile. "You're very forthright today," she observed.

"I'm interested, is all," Ryushi replied.

"My heartstone," she said, forsaking her previous inclination and sitting down on the bench next to him. She toyed with the three turquoise stones that lay against her collarbone, a larger one flanked by two smaller siblings, suspended between two thin silver chains.

"Your heartstone," he repeated flatly.

"Oh yes," she said. "I suppose I thought it was a simple gift, once. But then, I doubt it. I knew what I was doing. I knew the price. My father would go to any lengths to bribe affection out of me, but I don't think even he expected I would take him up on the chance to have the Keriags."

"The Keriags?" Ryushi asked, suddenly very interested. At that moment, a mercenary thought leaped to the forefront of his mind; if Aurin trusted him, had he not accomplished what dozens of Parakka spies had not been able to achieve? To get close to the Princess? And wasn't it his duty to his friends to exploit that?

But Aurin went on, conversationally, blithely unconcerned with what she was telling him. "The Keriags. See this big central stone here? My heartstone. Every Keriag Queen has a different stone implanted in their bodies, yes? If I take this off, within a cycle, every one of them will die. And so will the whole Keriag race."

Ryushi was dumbstruck. "I don't. . ." he began, then couldn't finish. The enormity of what she had just said, and the casual way she said it, choked off the sentence.

"It's quite simple," she said, brushing back one of the coils of her black hair over her bare shoulder. "A heartstone is cut from a much bigger gem, and many smaller offspring stones are taken at the time of its carving. In the same way that spirit-stones are attuned to the substance they affect, so the heartstone is attuned to its wearer's body. Their *aura*, I suppose you'd say. If it is removed from the beat of my heart for longer than a cycle or so, it cracks. And so do the offspring stones, which reside in the bodies of the Keriag Queens. And that kills them, yes?"

"But how did they . . . how did they *get* there?"

"My father. The Keriags have to come out to collect water for their fungus-gardens. He poisoned the water, and hence the gardens. Within cycles, the whole hive was incapacitated, and that was when he took the Queen and had her implanted. The Keriags share a hive-mind, and that includes the various Queens. Once one was done, the others could not voluntarily allow her to die; it would be like a man cutting off his own arm. So they, too, had to submit to the implants."

Ryushi was reeling. "And . . . you mentioned a price."

She nodded. "It's as you said; if you rule by fear, you can't ever stop. How can I take it off now? The Keriags would know the moment I did; and a cycle is plenty of time for them to swarm. They would home in on the heartstone and find me, and either make me put it back on or kill me."

"Couldn't you just take it off and leave it here, and go with the Jachyra through the mirrors to hide elsewhere? They'd never find you in time then."

"I *could*," she said. "That possibility is what keeps the Keriags in line; that is why they obey me. But how can I do that? I would keep the breath in my body; but I would lose my *life*. Without the Keriags, I could not rule. I would have to forsake everything I have, yes? I care nothing for the lands I have been given; but how could I go from this," – here she made a motion that encompassed everything beyond the walls of the cell – "to poverty? And who knows what my father would do if he ever found me?"

"What about him? Couldn't you . . . use the Keriags against him?" Ryushi ventured, hardly even daring to hope.

Aurin laughed, high and clear. "You think he would have got to where he is if he didn't think of things like that? No, Father was clever. He knew, if he gave me the Keriags, I could use them against him if ever I felt the inclination; and there are many more Keriags than Guardsmen. He might profess that he loves me, but he is not stupid. No, this heartstone is linked to the trigger-stone in his forehead; just like the Jachyra and his top-ranking aides have implanted stones that can kill them if they get out of line. If he dies, the heartstone will react as if I had taken it off. Within a cycle, the Keriags will die. Nothing can stop that, and the Keriags know it. They will not raise weapons against him. They would not even try and capture him; they dare not risk that he might take his own life before they could stop him." She gave a shallow sigh. "He knows I'd never turn against him. . ." Looking into Ryushi's horror-stricken eyes, she shrugged. "So really, I have no power at all. It is simply a circle, keeping both myself and the Keriags in check."

"Can't you reverse it somehow?"

Aurin smiled pityingly. "There are ways. A Deliverer could do it. Presumably my father intends to deactivate his trigger-stone when he gets old, to pass on the legacy of the Keriags to me after his death. But how could I set the Keriags free now? It comes back again to what you said; ruling by fear. If I reversed what my father had done, the Keriags would turn against me and kill me in revenge. Nothing could stop that."

Ryushi looked down at his feet. Now he saw

the trap that Aurin had stepped into; gaining the great strength of the Keriag race, in return for being tied inextricably into their fate. To have the dilemma of sacrificing everything for her freedom from the heartstone, or holding on to all the privileges that royalty offered her in return for staying in that trap. But then, it was plain that she did not *want* what Ryushi would call freedom. That was the gulf between them. She was happy to keep the power and the price, rather than forsake her royal life and its privileges. Macaan had banked on that, on her fear of poverty after a life of riches, and that was why she would never give it up.

Ryushi had been staring at the floor for a time; now he looked up at the Princess, and he was shocked to see a tear sliding down one porcelain cheek. He met the watery pools of her eyes as she spoke again, her voice full of sorrow.

"We have found the Parakkan base, Ryushi. Spies are being sent to confirm it, and on their return, all my forces will mobilize. In thirty cycles, maybe less, it will all be over."

Ryushi felt ice slide through his veins.

"I'm sorry," she said, and then leaned over and kissed him, lightly, on the lips. He told himself after she left that it was shock at her pronouncement that had led him to let her do it; but that was only a partial truth. He had wanted her to, despite everything.

It was about a cycle later when the door of his cell opened, and Ryushi looked up, an odd eagerness in his eyes; but the gaze turned to puzzlement as he saw a tall, grizzled man walk in instead of Aurin. The man turned and told the sentry to wait further up the corridor, and instructed that nobody else was to be admitted.

"Not even the Princess?" the sentry asked, his surprise muffled by the voice-grilles of his face-visor.

"As if the Princess would let you stop her," he said, the words thick with scorn. "Of course it doesn't apply to the Princess." But then, Gerdi thought to himself, it was hardly likely that the Princess Aurin would be along personally to visit her prisoners, now was it?

The door was closed and locked, and Ryushi

was on his feet, asking what this was all about, when the tall man turned round and he was suddenly no longer a man at all, but a boy, small and green-haired and wearing a wry grin on his face.

"You," he said, wagging a finger, "are a hard man to find."

"Gerdi!" Ryushi whispered in amazement. "I don't believe it!"

"Yeah, well," the Noman boy said modestly. "Believe it, 'cause they sent the best."

Ryushi impulsively reached out and hugged him, and Gerdi squirmed in his grip, embarrassed by the display of affection. "You came all the way in here—"

"– to get you, yeah, yeah. Only 'cause your sister would have killed me if I hadn't. Or that Calica chick; now *she's* been going spare while you've been away. What've you been up to there, huh?"

Ryushi looked up at the door, letting his jibe pass. "Listen, you've got to get out of here. Someone could come."

"Alright," he said. "Now here's the plan. We—"

"Gerdi," Ryushi said, holding up his hand. "Gerdi, wait. I can't go with you."

Gerdi blinked, then decided that he hadn't heard what he had just thought he had, and carried on talking. "Anyway, we go out into the corridor, and I pretend that I'm taking you to—"

"You're not *listening*," Ryushi hissed. "I can't go with you."

Gerdi narrowed his eyes. "You'd better have one giant-sized reason for what you've just said, 'cause let me tell you I have had a *bad* time of it recently."

"I've got *two* giant-sized reasons," came the reply. "One: Aurin's found Base Usido, and in less than thirty cycles from now she'll hit it with the full force of her armies. She's just waiting for confirmation from her spies, then she'll mobilize. And two: I know how she controls the Keriags. What I don't know is what I can do about it."

Gerdi and he hunkered down together. "Talk fast, Ryushi," said the Noman boy. "I need a lot of explaining done real quick."

So Ryushi told him about Aurin's heartstone, and how it was linked to the Keriag Queens, and how it would crack if it was taken away from her heartbeat for more than a cycle. And he told him about how Macaan had put down the Keriags before, and about how Aurin told him they had discovered the Parakkan Base, and about –

"*What?*" Gerdi almost shouted, but caught himself at the last moment and dropped his voice to a loud hiss. "Don't even think about it, Ryushi. It's *Aurin* we're talking about here! You can't—"

"I didn't say *I* was in love with *her*," Ryushi said, the embarrassed heat in his face gathering as he spoke. "I think that *she* loves *me*."

"Tell me you don't return the compliment," Gerdi said, his eyes narrowed suspiciously.

Ryushi paused, caught for a moment, then decided not to answer. "Look, that's not important at the moment," he said. "We've tried for ages to get spies on the inside of this place, people close to Aurin who could find this stuff out! I mean, about the Keriags . . . I just *asked* her and she *told* me."

Gerdi looked at him, his impish face frozen in disbelief.

"I've been thinking," Ryushi said. "Ever since Aurin told me about the Base, a cycle or so ago. I can *get* that heartstone. But *you* need to figure out how to stop it killing the Keriags, and how to stop the Keriags killing her."

"What for? Let 'em both die. Unless you *are* sweet on Aurin?" He said this last in a scornful, half-mocking tone.

"I am *not* gonna be part of the murder of an entire *species*," Ryushi hissed. "And besides, how much damage do you think the Keriags can do in a single cycle? If we destroy the heartstone, you can be sure they'll take us with them."

"Nice and small task you've just lumped on me, then," Gerdi said sulkily.

"You got a better idea?"

"Yes! I get you out of here and then we evacuate Base Usido!"

"And then we're right back where we started! Except we're even worse off; we'll have nothing to build with, no equipment, nothing. We might as well just stay where we are and be massacred."

Gerdi was silent, gazing levelly at his friend in the torchlight.

"Look, there's something else. Aurin's been telling me about these dreams she has. The person she describes in them is *Calica*; but

Aurin's never met her, and she doesn't know her."

Gerdi's eyes lit up. "Wait, wait. Kia said something about that, after her trial with the Koth Taraan."

"Her what?"

"I'll tell you later. But she kept on seeing Aurin and Calica together, and she didn't know why. And *Calica* was talking, too; she said she hadn't been sleeping well lately. Might be 'cause she's been having dreams. . ." He paused, then looked up at Ryushi. "Is that the best connection you've got?"

"Best and only."

"Good enough for me. Whatcha wanna do?"

Ryushi broke into a smile. "Okay. Now you know about the heartstone and what it does, you can work out how to get around it. I'll stay here. When the time comes, I'll be in the right place to snatch it, or whatever. Parakka have got to do something, and do it *now*. I think that taking out the Keriags is the only way they can win."

"You'd take the Princess's heartstone? Listen, if you say you're gonna do it, you'd better *do* it."

"I'll do it," he replied. "All you've got to do is

guarantee me that if you make a move, and I snatch that necklace, you have a way to deactivate it or get rid of it or *something*. Within a cycle or less."

"Got it," Gerdi said. "You know, Kia's gonna turn me inside out when she finds out about this. If Calica doesn't get me first."

"That's tough," Ryushi replied. "The way I figure it, there's only one way you can go. And that's this way. Attack is the only option; hit the palace by surprise. We can't run any more."

"You make me this promise, before I go," Gerdi said, turning suddenly grave. "You're close to the Princess, right? Maybe you're closer to her than you say. Well, promise me this. Whatever it takes, *whatever* it takes, you remember who your friends are. And if that means tearing that thing off her neck and stamping on it, then you do that. If the whole of the Keriag race goes down and Princess Aurin with it, that's fine by me. But don't even *think* about putting her in front of us if it comes to the choice."

Ryushi was taken aback by the change in the usually jovial Gerdi. "I . . . I . . ."

"*Promise* me," he said, and for a moment it was Banto crouching there, speaking those words, reminding Ryushi of a promise he made a lifetime ago to his dead father: to protect Elani, whatever the cost. The only thing he had left of the man was that promise, and he realized then that if he did not agree to what Gerdi said, then he was breaking it. And nothing was strong enough to make him do that.

He didn't know if it was Gerdi or his own mind that had conjured the image, but as they stood up from where they had been squatting, he bowed his head.

"You've got my promise," he said.

"Great," said Gerdi, suddenly smiling. "Now, the perk." He rummaged in his pocket and drew out a small key. "Thought they'd have to keep your powers down somehow, so I got this. I bet you're real sick of your Damper Collar by now, right?"

Outside, under the black, hollow eye of the Kirin Taq sun, the sky was clear, belying the storm to come.

4

A Cancer in the Web

Deep in the Rifts, the residents of Base Usido were counting the cost of their victory.

The Snagglebacks and Snappers, following the disappearance of the Banes that controlled their pack leaders, had suddenly found themselves without direction. Most of the leaders were killed by the shock of having the Banes leave their bodies; those few that were not became disorientated and confused. Whatever communication went on between the leaders and their packs faltered, and the creatures dissolved into panic and disorder. The Parakkans, seeing their chance, leaped on the routed army and drove them away, pushing them back across the plains where they scaled the cliffs and scattered into the forest. Those creatures that had got inside the perimeter wall were similarly robbed of purpose and organization, and the troops had wiped them out with relative ease after that.

But the Base had been crippled. Huts had been destroyed, vital machinery wrecked by the Snagglebacks' powerful fists. The small hatchery that they had maintained was beyond repair. Some of the grain silos were ruptured, and the grain would spoil. At least the small vehicles that they had left had remained undamaged. But the dead . . . the dead numbered perhaps a quarter of the Base's population. Broken bodies lay on the bluish grass, twisted and torn, their eyes staring after their departed essences. Men, women and children; Kirin and Dominion-folk alike.

"Funny," said Calica, as she sat next to Hochi and surveyed the clean-up effort. "All this time, we were worried about Aurin finding the Base. And it turns out to be the land itself that got us. I guess we underestimated the danger of building a Base in the Rifts."

"It was that, or nothing," Hochi said grimly, bowing his head. "If not for Aurin's tyranny, we wouldn't *have* to hide. This was the only place we could build in secret without her finding us."

"So now what?" Calica said, brushing her orange-gold hair back over her shoulder. A moment later, she answered her own question. "We rebuild, I suppose. Start again. Make sure we do sweeps for Bane more regularly. Work out a way to keep them out."

"I suppose," Hochi agreed without enthusiasm, his small eyes dark under his heavy brow, ranging over the destruction around him. He was weary of war, tired of the killing. He had seen too much to feel horror at the death that surrounded them; so had Calica. But he was tired, *so* tired, of struggling against a seemingly impossible enemy only to face setback after setback. "The fight goes on," he said to nobody, and the words seemed to have no force behind them.

Calica turned her olive eyes to the ground. She knew how he felt. Sometimes it felt like they were living a fool's dream, thinking that they could change anything. The power of Macaan and Aurin was too great; what could a motley group of idealists ever do against such an implacable enemy? So they could turn around a few people, make them see the Parakkan point of view instead of Macaan's indoctrination. So what? What did it really matter? They weren't achieving anything unless they could follow their talk up with action. And how could they do that now? Every time they looked like they were making progress, they were cut down again.

Sometimes she felt like just throwing it all in. But there was only one thing stopping her; and that was the fact that there was no other choice. She couldn't live as a happy citizen of an empire that had killed her parents and orphaned her. So the only alternative was to oppose that empire, and hope to bring it down.

But it was so heartbreakingly *hard*.

She looked up as Elani, Jaan and Iriqi approached from across the blood-darkened grass. It was an odd sight, to see the two Parakkans followed by the hulking creature, over twice their size. Neither of the young humans took much notice of the carnage around them. Calica felt a sudden stab of sorrow; their innocence and childhood had been just another casualty of the war that had enveloped their lives.

If Iriqi felt something, she could not read it on its alien features.

They walked up and joined Calica and Hochi, the slight wind stirring their hair, carrying the smell of oily smoke and dirty blood.

"Shouldn't you be helping with the clean-up?" Calica asked Elani.

"Shouldn't you?" Elani countered. Calica shrugged as the girl hopped up next to her. It seemed that the lowering of spirits was universal in Base Usido, and the usual pulling-together attitude of the Parakkans had faltered.

"How are you finding humankind, Iriqi?" she asked the Koth Taraan, her voice heavy with irony.

((We are distressed by what has occurred here. The younger Brethren believe it is similar to what will happen to our home if Macaan is not checked. The Koth Macquai has been given cause to think again about his policy of non-involvement))

"Nothing like a demonstration to really bring a point home, is there?" Calica said, but she sounded too weary to make the effort at sarcasm.

((I am sorry for your loss)) Iriqi said, and a

powder-blue cloud of plaintive sorrow glowed in their minds.

"How do you *do* that?" Elani asked, looking quizzically at the hulking creature.

"It's their way of expressing themselves," Jaan said in its place. "They don't have any features, or a mouth, so they project their emotions instead." He patted Iriqi's armoured foreleg in a companionable way. "Iriqi's only young. It hasn't quite mastered restraint yet, so whatever it's feeling comes out when it talks. The older Koth Taraan can hold back their colours so as not to give themselves away to strangers like us."

Calica blinked. She didn't think she'd ever heard Jaan speak at such length before. Iriqi, obviously deciding that the answer had already been given well enough, did not say anything. It just gazed at them with its huge, black eyes.

"What happened to the Banes?" Hochi asked Iriqi suddenly. "It *was* you, wasn't it?"

((The Bane that Jaan and I met in the caves sensed the Communion that binds the Koth Taraan together. Like us, it can see the links that are invisible to human eyes. It did not

understand what it sensed, because it had never encountered one of us before. But it desired it. It tried to enter my body, in the same way that they enter human bodies))

"Yeah, we know that *now*," Calica said, thinking of the little boy, Paani, who had opened the gate and let the hordes inside.

The Koth Taraan shifted and settled into its neutral stance. *((As it entered me, every one of my Brethren turned their attention to expelling it. The Communion will not abide a cancer in the web. The reaction was immediate and instinctive. But the Bane, too, are linked as we are; and the backlash from the destruction of the one who tried to possess me travelled to the rest of the Bane and annihilated them))*

"The Bane are gone, then?" Calica asked, faint hope in her voice.

((Dispersed)) Iriqi said. *((They cannot be destroyed entirely. They will reform, in time))*

Calica's shoulders slumped. "Then we can look forward to a repeat performance of today."

"You think *that's* bad," said a voice from behind them. "Wait'll you hear *this*."

"Gerdi?" Hochi cried, turning around. There, on the other side of the log fence that they had been sitting on, the green-haired Noman boy grinned at them.

"In the flesh," he said, but his breath was suddenly robbed as Hochi swung off the fence and gathered him up in a bear hug.

"Mauni's Eyes, Gerdi, I thought you wouldn't be coming back!" he said, his face a picture of joy.

"Not . . . sure . . . I wanna . . . *be* back," Gerdi gasped, struggling in the crushing circle of Hochi's massive arms. He half-suspected that the big man was hugging him a little too hard on purpose, for putting him through all that worry. "Let me *go* already!"

"Where's Ryushi?" Calica asked, desperate worry on her face. "Is he okay?"

Gerdi prised himself out of Hochi's arms and then looked around the assembled faces. "Someone get Kia. She's gonna want to hear this."

Gerdi would not speak until they were all assembled, and he did not want them to be distracted, so he arranged for them to meet in the ruined shell of the wyvern hatchery. The furnaces were quiet now, and the heat had dispersed through the great tear in the roof, the result of an explosion where a Snaggleback had smashed a fuel pod. Most of the eggs were undamaged, but they lay cold in their metal cradles, never to hatch now. It was deserted inside, and the ring of their boots on the floor grilles echoed through the massive chamber. The few glowstones that had not been shattered in the explosion threw their faint orange cast across the faces of those who gathered there, small figures in the near-dark.

"Get on with it, Gerdi," Kia snapped. "We don't need the theatrics. You could have just told us outside."

"You're lucky I'm here to tell you at all," Gerdi replied. "I've got a lot to say, and I don't want someone trying to rope you into corpse-mopping duty while I'm doing it, okay? Now shut up and listen." If his customary good humour seemed to have run a little dry of late, then nobody could blame him; he had been having a hard time of it recently, and there was little that even he could laugh about.

So they fell silent, and he began to speak. He told them that Ryushi was well, and that he remained a prisoner in Fane Aracq. He told them that he seemed to be in no immediate danger, and how he had managed to prise delicate information out of Aurin; but he did not say anything of his suspicions about Ryushi's feelings for the Princess or of her feelings for him. He glanced guiltily at Calica as he glossed over that part, but she was too taut with concern for Ryushi to notice.

He told them that Aurin knew where the Base was, and that she was readying her forces to wipe out Parakka once and for all. He told them also that Aurin's heartstone was the key to her control of the Keriags, but that it could not be removed without the death of the entire Keriag race and, most probably, Aurin herself. And he told them of Ryushi's resolution to stay, and his plan, and how he had charged Gerdi with finding a way to stop the murderous effects of the heartstone.

"The idiot!" Kia cried, raging. "What does he care about the Keriags, or Aurin? He should just steal it from her and let them all die; then Parakka might have a chance! Without the Keriags, Aurin's power in Kirin Taq would collapse. There'd be a revolution within a few cycles!"

"It's hardly that simple," said Hochi. "He can't exactly just walk up to her and take it." He looked at Gerdi and sighed heavily. "This news could not have come at a worse time. Our Base is poorly defended, our manpower is down; and now we are told that Aurin is soon to be on her way and that our only chance of winning is to attack her."

"I seem to remember a similar tactic a year ago," Calica said. "It didn't work then. It won't work now."

"What if she's *lying?*" Elani piped up suddenly, cutting them all dead. "You know, like Aurin's feeding him false information or something. Maybe they *let* Gerdi in so we'd panic and run and then we'd—"

"Hey, nobody *lets* me in anywhere!" Gerdi huffed, indignant. "If you knew *half* of what I had to go through to get to Ryushi, you wouldn't be so—"

"She does have a point, Gerdi," Jaan said softly. "Did she actually tell him the location, or just that she'd found it?"

Gerdi ruffled his hair with one hand, the green turned yellow in the orange light. "I don't know. I didn't exactly have time to chat with him about the particulars."

"The heartstone could be a bluff, too," Calica pointed out, her olive eyes steady.

"It could *all* be a bluff," Gerdi said. "But Ryushi doesn't think so, and right now he's the only thing we've got to rely on. Now we can argue whether Aurin was telling the truth or not all night, but what it comes down to is that we've gotta have some faith in him. 'Cause if what he says is true, then we've got one chance to get ourselves out of this or we're all dead."

There were a few moments of silence following his pronouncement. The assembled band of Parakkans looked at each other in the flat light, and listened to the metallic emptiness of the hatchery.

"Why didn't you go to the Council with this?" Kia asked.

"The Council will take too long. I'm not here to debate with anyone, anyway. I'm just telling you what I know."

"What are we gonna do?" Elani asked.

72

"Well, that depends." Gerdi flicked his eyes to Calica. "Ryushi said you had something to do with it."

"With what?" Calica asked, taken aback.

"The heartstone. Aurin's been having dreams about you. Kia says she kept seeing you and Aurin together in her vision. Have you been dreaming about Aurin?"

The question was bluntly put, and Calica had no other answer but the truth. "Yes," she said.

"So what's the connection?" Gerdi demanded.

"There *is* no connection! We've never met!" Calica cried. "Except when I touched Macaan's mind, that time. That was when it started."

Calica's comment sent their minds back to the time just before the Integration, back in the sunlight of the Dominions. It seemed so long ago now for those who were present when Calica used her power of psychometry on Macaan's earring to divine the mind and plans of the person who wore it. She had also come across previously unguessed aspects of the King's life, such as his fierce and unrequited love for his daughter and his fear of the death that had carried off his queen and his parents.

*((**You do have a connection**))* Iriqi said suddenly.

Jaan looked up at the great creature. "Does she?" he asked in surprise.

*((**I do not know the nature of the link. But they are connected. A single shared bond hangs between them**))*

"You can *see* that?" Elani asked, fascinated.

*((**Not as you see. But it is there, human child**))*

"How can I have a . . . a *connection* with her?" Calica cried. "What have we got in common?"

Elani scratched the back of her ear. "You're Splitlings, aren't you?" By the tone of her voice, it was less of a question, more of an obvious statement.

"Don't be stupid!" Calica replied, a look approaching panic on her face.

Elani looked at her pityingly, adopting once more a voice belonging to someone much older than she was. "Reports say she's about the same age as you. She was most likely born in Kirin Taq; you were born in the Dominions. Remember, back on Os Dakar, I told you about the greatest philosophers of Kirin Taq and the Dominions?

Baan Ju and Muachi? How they were Splitlings, each one balancing the other in the cosmic order just like Kirin Taq balances our homeland?" She paused, and then smiled. "I think you've just found your Splitling."

"That's a lie!" Calica almost shouted, her hair whipping around her face as she looked from Elani to Iriqi and back again.

"You had contact with her through Macaan's memories when you touched the King's earring. Even though you didn't realize it, you found your bond. And subconsciously, you've been keeping it alive ever since. Through your dreams."

"And what I saw in the vision. . ." Kia said, caught up in the thrust of communal deduction. "The Koth Taraan said that the trial could bring up insights I didn't know I had, or premonitions. It was telling me about Calica and Aurin! That's why they were always together!"

Was *that* the reason behind Kia's lasting dislike of Calica? She had thought it was jealousy, that she was taking up the attentions of her twin, but had she *known*, somehow, deep down, that –

"Shut *up*!" Calica cried, turning on her. "Stop

making decisions about me! What, you're gonna listen to a nine-winter kid who thinks she's solved the mysteries of the universe? And something that isn't even the same *species* as us? All this stuff about Splitlings is just a bunch of Resonant myth! I'm nothing to do with Aurin and I never will be! It was her family that killed my *parents*!"

She shoved Kia aside and stormed away, her hurried steps clacking through the still air of the hatchery until she stepped through the small, dim rectangle of the workers' entrance and was gone.

"She's in denial," Elani said confidently, putting a finger on her lips.

"Forget that for a minute," Kia said, suddenly seeming energized by the idea that had come to her. "You've been coming up with all kinds of theories about stuff like Splitlings, haven't you?"

"You wanna hear some, Cousin Kia?" Elani asked, beaming.

"I wanna know if a Splitling can fool a heartstone."

Dead silence.

"Replace Aurin with Calica?" Hochi said after

the implications of what she had just said had
been given adequate time to sink in.

"Get the heartstone off the Princess," Kia said.
"Put it on Calica." She clicked her fingers, the
loud snap dissolving into the recesses of the dim
chamber. "We have the Keriags. And it's no more
Macaan. The *worst* that can happen is we destroy
the heartstone and the Keriags die."

"You're *that* sure Iriqi's right?" Elani asked.

"Listen: when I saw Takami in those visions, he
was missing an ear. I didn't know why then; now
I've been hearing reports and rumours from the
spies that Ryushi cut it off during their duel. What
I saw in the Koth Macquai's pool was genuine. If
it was right about Takami, it'll be right about
Calica and Aurin."

"I'm not sure slavery is part of Parakka's ethic,"
Gerdi commented, remembering what Ryushi had
said. "Or mass genocide, for that matter."

Kia shot him a scathing look, then grabbed
Elani by the shoulders. "*Would it work?*" she
demanded.

Elani looked confused for a moment. "Well,
yeah, sure, I guess it *might*. Heartstones don't care

about the pace of the heartbeat, 'cause that would go faster and slower with exercise and sleep and stuff. They're tuned in to the person's aura."

"Do Aurin and Calica share the same *aura*, then?" Kia asked in exasperation, her green eyes urgent.

"Well, you gotta look at it like this," said the little girl, pulling away from Kia's grip – which was beginning to hurt a little – and moving back a step. "See, twins like you and Ryushi share a lot of physical stuff, but you're *totally* different in, like, spiritual ways. Personality and attitude and so on. So you have different auras. Splitlings are the other way around. Physically, they have nothing in common except the time of their birth, 'cause that's when the bond forms. But their aura, their core being, is the same." She shrugged. "I got most of this from the old writings that we saved from other Resonants. Maybe Aurin's what Calica would have been if their situations were different. Certainly explains why Ryushi's in love with both of them."

"*What?*" Kia and Gerdi chorused together.

Elani gave the Noman boy a sad smile. "Oh,

come *on*, Gerdi. You gave *so* much away. And apart from that, how else would Ryushi find out all that stuff? You never explained that, did you? And as for *Calica*, you'd have to have less eyes than a Snaggleback not to see that one." She paused. "Though I'm not sure if Ryushi knows it himself yet," she mused thoughtfully.

Gerdi's jaw dropped. Elani had always displayed the ability to come up with some staggering insights, but she had nailed him so convincingly this time that he was beginning to think she was nothing short of psychic.

"He is *not* in love with Calica!" Kia cried, even though she had suspected it for some time. "And he is *certainly* not in love with Aurin." She turned on Gerdi, anger written on her face. "*Is* he, Gerdi?"

Gerdi swallowed, his eyes moving nervously over her features, before breaking into a sheepish grin. "Errr . . . I was kinda holding that one back," he admitted.

"He *told* you?"

"He didn't *say*, but I got my suspicions."

"Oh, that's just *great*!"

"Isn't it, though?"

"Shut up!"

Gerdi shrugged. "If you can't *handle* it. . ."

"Stop this, all of you!" Hochi roared suddenly, raising his huge hands to quiet them. They all looked at him, his enormous belly and bald head limned in orange light. When he had their attention, he went on.

"Now I don't have much in the way of words, and I don't have the smarts that some of you have—"

"You got *that* right," said Gerdi; but Hochi had anticipated a clever comment from the boy, and sent a pre-emptive strike his way. Gerdi had barely finished his sentence and was preparing to dodge when a cuff struck him off-guard and sent him flying into the darkness.

"But I know what's important, and that's what counts here," Hochi continued. "Now Aurin *may* have been lying, but there's one thing we can say is looking pretty likely. And that is that we have Aurin's Splitling here with us. Ryushi is relying on us to get him out of there, don't forget. He had in mind an attack on Fane Aracq. In the confusion, he would get the heartstone. Right, Gerdi?"

"Right," Gerdi replied, getting up and rubbing the back of his head; but the string of mumbled insults that followed his agreement were a little too quiet to be heard.

"Now think about it. Kia, you say he should snatch the heartstone and be done with it. That's no good. He would be killed before he could escape, and the heartstone returned to Aurin. So we need an attack, an attack strong enough to break into Fane Aracq."

"The Keriags," Kia said. "But we can't get the stone without the Keriags, and we can't get the *Keriags* without the stone."

"Maybe we can," said Jaan. He was looking at his huge companion.

((You are suggesting that we communicate with the Keriags)) Iriqi said, a pale shiver of distaste riding shotgun.

"You can't communicate with the Keriags!" Kia said.

((The Keriags are intelligent beings. They can communicate)) the Koth Taraan said, shifting uneasily. It turned its huge, black eyes on Jaan. *((You will ask me to do this thing, won't you?))*

"You have to, Iriqi," said Jaan. "For all of us. It's our only chance."

"Will the Koth Macquai allow you to?" Kia asked.

((It leaves the decision to me. It is my choice))

"Will you?" Jaan pleaded. "I know how you all feel about the Keriags, but—"

"Whoa, hang on here," said Gerdi, waving his hands. "You're actually suggesting going to *talk* with the Keriags?"

"To cut a deal," Hochi said in his deep bass voice. "They help us storm Fane Aracq and get the stone. We free them from their slavery."

Gerdi slowly covered his face with his hand. "I don't believe I'm hearing this," he said, the words muffled by his palm.

5

Blind Trust Alone

"Err . . . so explain again why I got volunteered for this when I got one of the long straws," Peliqua said in puzzlement, lying on her stomach on a small hillock of dark blue grass.

"Just lucky, I guess," Kia replied. "Now keep it quiet, or you'll get heard."

In the dimness of Kirin Taq, they lay peering over the rim of their hiding place. All around them, tiny flowers bloomed, their translucent, crystalline petals trapping the feeble light from the black sun overhead and reflecting it endlessly inward. Glimmer plants shone green, pinpricks of light that clustered in bunches against the darker hills all around.

Before them was a Ley Warren, rising out of the land to scratch the sky, its irregular earthen towers like huge, misshapen fingers. It was not unlike the structure south of Tusami City in the Dominions; unsupported walkways crisscrossed between the tall towers, and the base was a mass of ramps and tunnels for the Keriags and the Guardsmen to get in and out. It was an enormous termitary, stretching towards the clouds, and crawling with the black, insectile forms of the Keriags.

The Ley Warrens. When they had first appeared in the Dominions over a year ago, they had been a mystery. They had turned out to be the linchpin of Macaan's Integration; huge Keriag warrens surrounding Ley Boosters, the machines that created a bridge between Kirin Taq and the Dominions. The Ley Warrens existed in both worlds at once, passing-places for Macaan's men, guarded fiercely by the Keriags.

Kia watched the creatures for a time. She didn't need a spyglass to remind herself what they looked like. Humanoid torsos, slung low between six chitinous, spiderlike legs that angled upwards from their ribs and then bent back down at the knee-joint. Their bodies covered in horny spikes of armour; their eyes small and black beneath their jutting eye-ridges. And each carrying a *gaer bolga*, a short spear with backward-facing serrations to rip and tear at an enemy's flesh as it was pulled out.

Hard to believe that they were distant relatives of the Koth Taraan. The onyx eyes, the armour . . . but that was where the similarity ended.

She hoped that this was going to work; because they were taking an awful chance with their plan. Would Iriqi even be able to communicate with a Keriag? Would it respond? And what then? What did they have to offer the Keriags as assurance except theories and possibilities? Would the Keriags be willing to gamble with the extinction of their species for a chance to be free? And even if they *were* freed, what then? Would they rampage across the faces of both worlds, destroying everything?

They had no other choice, so she put it out of her mind. It was the only thing she could do.

"Oh! Oh! Kia!" Peliqua said excitedly, nudging her. "Here it comes."

It had taken them a short while to study the patrol routes of this Ley Warren. Nestled as it was in a natural basin in the hills, it was easier to approach than the one on the plains south of Tusami City, so the inhabitants had compensated with a tight net of sentries that combed the landscape around the main structure. These comprised both Keriag and Guardsman patrols.

Kia and Peliqua weren't interested in the Guardsmen. It was the Keriags that they were waiting for. And now, as Peliqua pointed, Kia saw that their patience had at last been rewarded. A single Keriag was coming, rounding the shoulder of a nearby hill, each of its six legs moving independently of the others as it stalked along.

Kia swallowed, and exchanged a glance with Peliqua. "Let's do it," she said, and they suddenly scrambled to their feet and ran. The Keriag snapped its head around instantly, fixing them with its cold, cruel eyes. There was a moment's pause, and then it came for them.

Kia and Peliqua sprinted to where their pakpaks waited silently, the sudden thrill of the chase firing their bodies. They swung up on to their mounts and spurred them just as the Keriag skittered over the ridge of the hillock. They couldn't outrun a Keriag; but a pakpak could.

"*Go!*" Kia cried as she spurred her mount, and her pakpak took off with such a burst of acceleration that she was forced back in her saddle by the wind drag. Peliqua was close behind her, her red braids blowing around her face.

The Keriag was not far behind. The pakpaks were faster in a straight run, but the terrain was hilly and the Keriag's six legs carried it effortlessly over the uneven ground. Kia and Peliqua bolted down the hillock and into a shallow trench between two rocky hills, and the Keriag followed, moving with sure treads where the pakpaks skidded.

The hive-mind of the Keriag Queen in the Warren would know of them already. Probably, other Keriags were already heading from other directions to intercept them. The fact that they did not have far to ride did nothing to alleviate Peliqua's worry, as she saw the terrible black insect-thing come down the trench after her. One trip, one wrong foot, and it would all be over.

The rock walls suddenly gave way, receding back into the blue grass of the hills, and their narrow path opened into a stony clearing, a flat spot of neutral ground between three neighbouring hills. Kia broke left as she reached the clearing; Peliqua swung right, and then both wheeled around. The Keriag burst through after them . . . and stopped, utterly motionless and still.

((Greetings to you, Keriag))

Iriqi was there, in the centre of the clearing. Aside from Kia and Peliqua, there were also Jaan and Ty. Their weapons were drawn, but they were making no move to attack and were staying at a distance from the creature. All of them watched the Keriag, as if any of them could divine what it was thinking. The black of its eyes were fixed on the black of the Koth Taraan's.

((I am of the race of the Koth Taraan. We seek an audience with your Queen)) Iriqi was unable to keep the slight taint of disgust from the hue of the words.

Still the Keriag made no response. It stayed, motionless and poised, relaying what it saw back to the hive-mind and waiting to be told what to do. Kia looked nervously around the hills that surrounded the gravel clearing; other Keriags were beginning to arrive now, summoned by the plight of the first. The plan had been to get the attention of the Keriags without the Guardsmen noticing anything untoward; but they were getting an uncomfortable amount of attention right now. Were the Keriags just stalling them until they could get their warriors into place?

((Respond if you understand me, Keriag. We shared the same ancestor, once)) The Koth Taraan looked suddenly at Jaan, and then back to the Keriag. *((Our differences are superficial at best. We have not grown so far apart that we cannot share communication))*

Peliqua could not help a twinge of sadness, even in their present situation, as she caught that glance towards her brother. The smallest of moments, it spoke volumes about what was between them now, the creature and the halfbreed. Had that been why Iriqi had agreed to talk to the Keriags for them? Because of what Jaan had taught him, about how prejudices against race and species can be overcome? About how even a halfbreed, despised by both the races he was born from, has the same heart and soul as other people, even other *species*?

She knew that it had, and it pained her. For all of the protection, all of the self-esteem she had tried to give her brother, it had taken a creature that was not even human to give him the companionship he needed, and help strip away the shame and disgust that he felt for himself.

"Kia!" she said. "There's more of them coming. If we don't get out of here soon, I think we might be in a bit of trouble."

Kia sat up on her pakpak and looked around. The Keriags lined the three ridges above the clearing now, silhouetted against the velvet purple sky, their *gaer bolga* held low between their long, spindly legs. She felt prickly sweat begin to gather on her scalp. It would soon be time to make the call. If she left it too late, they might not get out alive. But if they fought now, they would lose any chance of talking to the Keriags; and that would mean the eventual destruction of Parakka. She set her jaw and watched the lone Keriag, and willed it to respond.

((We have a proposal)) said Iriqi. *((We can free you from the heartstone. All of you. But we need your help in return))*

There was a long silence. Then, in a voice like a thousand rats scratching at a metal door, the Keriag hive-mind replied.

<<<Follow us>>>

The Keriags had many different ways into and out of the Ley Warren, and the Guardsmen knew less than half of them. The labyrinthine tunnels were too complicated to be mapped by the human mind, and too numerous to be counted. They had underground paths that came out over a mile away from this particular Warren, and it was down these that the Parakkans were led. Their pakpaks had been left on the surface, and they had brought glowstones to fend off the darkness within those parts of the Warren that were not travelled by Guardsmen. But the light hardly lessened the terror that they felt as they trod the earthen corridors of the Keriags, surrounded by the skittering of hard, clawed feet and the hum of the Flow from the nearby Ley Booster.

Kia's throat was tight and she hardly dared to swallow. She had Ty's hand clutched tightly in hers, her eyes darting this way and that as the light of Ty's glowstone slid over a black carapace or a leg, reflecting a shine both dull and moist. They were utterly, totally, in the power of the Keriags now. There would be no way to fight out of this one, no miracle escape or last-minute rescue. They were deep in the heart of the enemy's territory, and all around them was an escort of creatures that could tear them apart in moments. Even Iriqi. The Koth Taraan was hardly helping matters, either; she was unable to get the icy black-blue of mortal fear out of her head, and she suspected this was a spill-over from Iriqi's own emotions.

But at least they were being granted an audience. That was something. However, that only posed new problems for her. For what she had to say was not something the Keriag Queen would want to hear. If Calica had come with them, maybe she could have handled it; but she had been forced to stay at Base Usido and try to coordinate some kind of response to the threat of Aurin's armies. So it was up to her, again. She had failed last time; why did they think that now would be any different?

She took a shuddering, nervous breath; Ty glanced at her and squeezed her hand, letting her know that he was there. She turned her thoughts to the offer she was to make the Keriag Queen. The Keriags were to help them besiege Fane Aracq; and in the meantime, her twin on the inside would steal the heartstone. The moment the heartstone was removed, the Keriags would know of it. They would then storm the palace, Ryushi would place the heartstone on Calica, and order would be restored. They could then work out how to deactivate the heartstone at their leisure, and Aurin's power would be shattered. For without the Keriags, she did not have enough of a force to hold Kirin Taq.

There were a hundred things that could go wrong. First, Calica's agreement to cooperate had been very reluctant; but that was a minor thing. Kia trusted that she would come through. She knew it was Ryushi's life at stake. She would do it for him. Secondly, they had no guarantee that the heartstone would be fooled by Aurin's Splitling. If it was not, then disaster would ensue. Thirdly, it was uncertain whether Ryushi could get the stone at all; that was going on blind trust alone. *Fourthly*, would the Keriags be happy about switching the stone to Calica? After all, they had no reason to trust her. If Calica chose to abuse her power, then they had simply swapped one mistress for another.

And was it wise to let the Keriags free at all? She didn't think so. She wanted them kept, so they could be used against Macaan in the Dominions. With the force of the Keriags at their command, they could wipe their homeland free of the stain of the tyrant King. But Calica was being terrifically stubborn about it; she refused even to consider Kia's point of view on the matter. Granted, it was selfish and unethical to use the Keriags as their slaves, but it would only be for a short time, and it was an action that had to be weighed against the thousands of lives they would save. Did Calica's decision have something to do with the antagonism between them? Probably, Kia thought bitterly. With this thing about being Aurin's Splitling, and the rumours that had reached her about Ryushi's feelings for the Princess, she was most likely doing it out of pique against the world.

She just had to rely on Ryushi. And hope that he was not really in love with Aurin, that Gerdi was mistaken somehow.

Now she felt sick. Why did everything have to revolve on such a tenuous thread? It was always the same; relying on the flimsiest of chances, hoping against hope that things would turn out alright. Well, this time she had a backup plan. For if the Queen did not agree to help her out, then she would threaten. Even in the heart of the Keriag lair, she would threaten.

Ryushi had made a promise to Gerdi. And in all the years they had been brother and sister, he had never broken a promise. If the Queen did not agree to Kia's offer, Parakka were going to attack the palace anyway. And Ryushi would destroy the heartstone. Somehow, in some way, he would do it or die trying. He had the power, now that Gerdi had fixed his Damper Collar. He could destroy a whole floor of the palace, if he needed to. And if he failed, someone else would try, and someone else, until eventually. . .

Now that Parakka knew about the heartstone, the Keriags were vulnerable. They could either join Parakka in an attempt to free themselves, or die with the Princess. Even if they took Parakka down with them, they would still die. That was the choice she would put to them. It was all bluff and uncertainty, but bluff and uncertainty were all she had right now. She would make out that they were far more confident than they really were, and hope that the Keriag Queen would not oppose them.

For if she did, they really had no hope at all.

The darkness, the scratches and scrapes seemed endless. They were moving in a bubble of their own light, able to see only what the edges of it brushed against; a tunnel wall, a retreating leg of a Keriag, other things less identifiable. All around them, uncomfortably close, were their escorts. It was terrifying to be so near to the creatures that they had fought with on Os Dakar and in the Ley Warren south of Tusami City, and the fear did not seem to recede but to increase as they were led deeper and deeper into trackless darkness. The air smelt dry and close, and seemed to press in on them hard from every side.

Eventually, the bare tunnels began to become

more varied, and they caught glimpses of side-caverns in which small Keriags busied themselves around fat white grubs the size of humans, who thrust their blind heads out of holes in the earthen wall where they appeared to live, and clamoured to be fed. They passed through one of the gardens that Ryushi and Elani had seen on their last foray into a Ley Warren, huge puffballs of multicoloured fungus that rustled and swayed in the light of white glowstones.

The presence of glowstones meant they were getting near the routes that humans trod, and Kia found herself getting uneasy. But *white* glowstones? Hadn't Ryushi seen the same thing in the other Warren? Perhaps the special light helped the fungus to grow. Maybe the Keriags had mined the stones themselves; they were certainly too expensive to obtain by other means.

They started to take an upsloping tunnel from the gardens, and then were suddenly turned off it and down a steep decline . . . and then, without warning, they were brought to a halt.

Darkness all around them, beyond the bubble of light. But they could sense, by the echoes of the tiniest of sounds, that they were in a cavern. A huge cavern. There were no tunnel walls visible now. Their Keriag escort retreated out of the range of their glowstones. And then there they were, alone, an island of reality in a void of infinite black nothingness, and only the whispers and scratches of the Keriags to indicate that there was anything outside their island at all.

And then there was a movement. Vast. And something enormous leaned forward from the darkness, so that the orange light shone in shaky lines across its jet-black carapace. Kia felt her stomach coil.

The Keriag Queen was nothing like her servants in appearance. Where they were thin, fast and deadly, she was monstrous and cumbersome, a huge thing with thousands of thick, millipede-like legs around the base of her body. She was protected by a pocked shell of chitin, with no visible break in her length, a dome of armour that surrounded her completely. Of her other organs, only her mouth was visible, a wide gash beneath the front lip of her armour, set on the underside of her body. She was like a whale that had adapted itself to the land, massive and blunt; and around her many legs and over her back raced many hundreds of the smaller Keriags, picking her clean, attending to her, washing her.

Nobody could speak.

The Keriag Queen shifted her immense weight, the movement like a miniature earthquake.

<<<Koth Taraan. Old Brethren. Keriags waited. You have come>>>

The speech was audible only to Iriqi, and he found it strangely welcoming.

((We have come)) he replied.

<<<Then speak>>> she said, and so it began.

Back at Base Usido, all was preparation. Calica strode among the chaos, directing a man here, giving orders there, overseeing the frantic operation that was underway. She knew that whatever they did would not be enough; it was just a question of maximizing their chances of survival for as long as possible.

It had long since been decided that evacuation was not an option. It was just impossible to get out of the Rifts at such short notice, due to the geography of the place. They would have to leave everything behind, and that would put them in an untenable position, leaving them defenceless for Aurin to hunt down. Besides, there was no place else to hide. And with the Snappers and Snagglebacks stirred up and roaming around, she didn't give much for the survival ratio of the Parakkans if they tried to move out *en masse.*

Standing and fighting. Well, if there was no other choice, then that was what they had to do. Most of the corpses of the previous attack had not been properly seen to yet, and they were beginning to smell bad; but they had to be ignored for the moment, while defences were prepared. She'd give them a few more cycles before the risk of disease would demand that they were disposed of.

Many of the fighters in the camp had already left, making their way through the hazardous forest to a rendezvous point on the northwest edge. From there they would receive word as to whether Kia's mission was successful or not; but if they heard nothing at all, they would go on regardless, to make a final, hopeless stab at Fane

Aracq in the hope that Ryushi could pull off something from the inside. If all went to plan, the Keriag Queen would send her troops – or at least a messenger – to the rendezvous point. Meanwhile, Kia and the others would return to take up the defence of Base Usido, for they could not possibly travel as fast as the Keriags from the Ley Warren, fast enough to rendezvous with the Parakkan forces in time. Calica herself was leaving in less than a cycle with Hochi and Gerdi to join the front line, to be the bearer of the heartstone if they were successful.

All they could do at Base Usido was hold out and hope that Aurin's troops did not reach them before Fane Aracq had fallen and the army had returned. If Ryushi's information was reliable, and all went to plan, then there would be just enough time. Their one chance was to get the first strike in, while Aurin was unaware that they knew. And after that . . . well, none of them could say. They could only survive. It was all that was left to them.

"I have bad news," said a flat voice by her shoulder, and she knew, somehow, that Anaaca was about to tell her something relevant to her thoughts.

"Aurin has sent her troops earlier than expected?" Calica asked, turning around.

Anaaca's expression was bland. "Nearly right." The spymistress watched her lazily for a moment, like a basking crocodile, before speaking again. "Takami is on the move. He's mobilized the forces of the province of Maar, and he's headed this way."

"Are you certain?"

"My spy in his court is sure. He has been in a rage for many cycles, since Ryushi took his ear. We can surmise that Aurin has told her thanes about the location of our Base, but she was waiting for her own spies to get here and confirm it. Rather like us, Takami has decided to jump the gun."

"Why?"

"Kia. Or so the nobles say. Ryushi is safe in Fane Aracq, so he wants to strike at the next best thing, the thing that will hurt him most. He thinks Kia is here."

"She will be, if she isn't killed by the Keriags first." Calica shifted her weight to her other leg.

"Do you really think Takami would risk his position as a thane in the name of revenge? That he is really that angry to have lost all reason?"

Anaaca examined her nails, painted a sharp red against the grey of her skin to match her hair. "Since his mutilation, he refuses to appear in court, and will allow nobody but his closest servants to see his face. Several retainers have been executed for offences that deserved little more than a reprimand."

Calica nodded thoughtfully. "How long before he gets here?"

"They're coming in on an awkward route, and it's not the shortest way either. Plus they'll be transporting weaponry and so on. Three cycles, probably."

"That'll be almost the same time as we hit Fane Aracq."

"Indeed."

Calica's eyes became focused on the middle distance, as if she was looking at something far away. "Then we can only hope our forces can fend him off until we return to help them."

"If we return at all."

She blinked, refocusing. "Thank you, Anaaca. You've been invaluable."

"I know," she replied, and with that she left.

Calica closed her eyes and rested her bunched fist on her mouth. It was an expression of deep thought and deeper sorrow. Things had gone from bad to worse, and she was one of those who was forced to deal with it. But she couldn't concentrate, she couldn't take it all, not with Ryushi imprisoned in their enemy's keep.

And not if the rumours were true. Not if the boy she loved felt the same for another woman. Aurin. Her Splitling.

She had missed her chance. Through pride, she had left it too late to declare her passion. And now just maybe she'd lost him for good.

She felt tears gathering behind her closed lids, but she drew in a sharp breath and swallowed them back, wiping her eyes. No. No weakness. Too many people were relying on her now.

Endure. Survive. Win. And that's all.

It was a mantra that she repeated to herself, over and over, as she walked away.

6

A Matter of Shades

The wyvern scythed through the purple sky, its forewings steering the airflow past its larger hindwings as it soared on the wind. On its back, a Rider lay in his harness, suited in his full-body armour of dark red. His face was a blank visor, with two dark eyepieces that scanned the ground far beneath him. Long black braids – the signature hairstyle of the King's Riders – streamed out from the crest of his helmet as he flew from Fane Aracq, the chaotic mass of white spikes and bubbles, parapets and cupolas becoming smaller with distance. It was his shift on patrol, here at the point where six provinces met, and so he led his two wingmen, beginning a long spiral across the lands, his flight path radiating outwards from the central point – the palace – and swinging wider and wider.

All was peace below him. The dark carpet of Kirin Taq spread out in a chequerboard of fields and roads under the black sun. Here and there, clusters of torchlight indicated towns or villages. Strips of Glimmer plants kept their ceaseless marking of time, faint smudges of red.

The Rider spiralled further away from the palace in a long, slow arc, his wingmen keeping abreast. His thoughts were not really on his patrol, but on other things; the upcoming assault, for one. Aurin had tried to keep it secret, but she couldn't hide the massing of troops being carried out at strategic points around Fane Aracq and the thanes' keeps. Something was going to happen, something *major*. It was only a matter of time.

He was curving south over the province of Dacqii when he noticed something odd. Far below him, against the deep blue-black of the twilit fields, there was movement. Actually, it looked almost as if the fields themselves were moving, undulating like the sea on a choppy day. He waved a gloved hand at his wingmen, indicating that he was about to descend, and then angled his wyvern towards the oddity. As he got closer, he frowned: what *was* it that he was seeing? The definition was too hard to hold on to, but it *looked* like. . .

His eyes widened in horror behind his mask.

The Keriags were swarming.

It was a dark cloud, spreading across the fields like ink, their black bodies almost invisible in the dim light. Thousands upon thousands of them, a stick-forest of ratcheting legs and jagged spears, eating up the ground beneath them as they moved with inhuman speed across the province. Heading towards the palace.

The sudden *whoomph* of a concussion-bolt made him flinch involuntarily, and the screech of one of his wingmen's wyverns sliced through his ears as it plummeted towards the all-consuming mass below, its Rider pawing the air desperately as he fell. He banked his own creature steeply as the sky suddenly came alive with force-cannon fire, fear flooding his veins. As if from nowhere, a fleet of wyverns had suddenly come up from beneath them, where they had been flying low to the ground, skimming the fields. Now, as his other wingman took a direct hit only a few metres away from him, he dug his fingers into the nerve-points on his wyvern – where the base of the neck met the shoulders of the forewings – and urged it forward hard. It complied with a screech, tearing away from the hail of force-bolts, dodging and swerving between the rippling trails of air distortion that they left behind them.

Parakka. Parakka were here, and there had been no warning. He had to get back to the palace, had to raise the alarm, had to –

He heard the report of the force-bolt as it launched even above all the others, as if some kind of sixth sense told him it carried his death with it. Blasted out of the sky, his wyvern dropped like a stone, trailing smoke and vapour behind it as it made its final descent.

The Keriags had been sighted leagues away from Fane Aracq on many occasions by the time they came into sight of the palace and the alarm went up. But still there had been no warning. Some that witnessed the swarm, villagers and townsfolk primarily, had learned through many hard lessons not to interfere in the Princess's business, and kept their heads down. Others would not have tried to warn the palace even if they could. Most ran home, locked their doors and bit their lips, hoping the swarm was not a harbinger of something awful. Any of the Princess's men that witnessed the horde suffered the same fate as the patrol Riders; outposts were overrun, vehicles were destroyed, Guardsmen were slain. But all of this was irrelevant, really, for only a wyvern could have possibly outrun the advancing force by far enough to make any difference. The Keriags were immensely fast, and they did not tire. In the end, the palace had only the slimmest of warnings – little over a half-hour in Dominion time – before the Keriags reached it.

The Keriags had poured from tunnels that the Princess had no idea existed, deep in the hills of Dacqii. The Keriags' subterranean network spanned a much greater area than anyone but they were aware of, and they still had their secrets, even in slavery. Aurin had sophisticated Machinist devices to warn her of any insurrection in the Ley Warrens; but she had never imagined that the Keriags could have managed to tunnel so close to Fane Aracq.

With them had come the Parakkans. Aurin was unaware of the damage that their forces had suffered at the hands of the Bane, and was similarly in the dark about how little machinery, vehicles and equipment they had. What she did not expect was a slimmed-down, mobile force of troops on pakpaks and wyverns, comprising little over a half of Parakka's fighting strength. They had been a small enough army to make their way through the sparsely populated Dacqii hills without being seen, and now formed the rearguard of the Keriag assault.

Nobody was ready for it. Nobody was prepared for an attack of such speed, during the moment when Fane Aracq was most vulnerable, when many of its troops were assembling elsewhere for the push into the Rifts. Nobody could have imagined it would be the Keriags.

The Queens had been waiting, waiting for a long time. Waiting for the Koth Taraan to arrive. Ever since Macaan had first tricked them, had exploited their hive-mind link with each other, they had suffered their bondage in silence.

Because they knew that, elsewhere, there were more of their kin. Those that Macaan did not know about, those who had hidden for centuries. The Old Brethren. The Koth Taraan.

The Keriags did not possess the eternal memory of the Koth Taraan. They did not hold on to the past, nor did they have anything like the Communion with which to pass on knowledge from one Queen to another. Their minds were always on the present, on the relentless industry of their colonies, seeing through thousands of different eyes at the same time. And whereas the Koth Taraan had cultivated emotion, even into creating expressive art, the Keriags had found it a hindrance to the efficient running of their colonies. Their emotions, except for the most rudimentary, had been allowed to wither and die, leaving them with only the most basic and primal of responses to interfere with their multi-minded reasoning.

But they remembered the Koth Taraan. It was not in a Keriag's nature to forget one of its own, even one separated by generations and centuries. The Koth Taraan and the Keriags had once been the same, before they had taken divergent paths and warred. The Koth Taraan had nurtured their grudges ever since, fearing and hating their distant brothers. The Keriags had forgotten why they fought a long time ago. To the Keriags, the Koth Taraan were still part of the hive, the great and ancient hive from which they all came.

And they had been waiting all this time. Waiting for their kin to come and free them from Macaan's yoke. After all, why wouldn't they? Wouldn't the Keriags do the same for them? Was that not kin? If a part of the hive was attacked, the whole hive went to its defence. That was the way the Keriags thought, the only way they knew *how* to think, and they could only assume that everything else thought the same way.

But they had waited, and waited, and the Koth Taraan had not come to their aid.

Until now.

The Parakkans had been taken aback by how instantly the Keriag Queen agreed with the plan put to them by Kia, through Iriqi. But if they had known the Keriag mind, it would not have surprised them. Trust was not a matter of shades of grey for a Keriag, it was absolute and total. A

Keriag could not conceive of one of its kin, even one as distant as the Old Brethren, lying to it or falsifying anything. If the Koth Taraan said it could be done, it could be done. That there was a margin for error did not matter to them. Their kin believed it would work, so they did too.

The day of their emancipation had come.

Deep inside Fane Aracq, Ryushi heard the wailing of a Machinist wind-siren and knew that it was time to act. The alarm was sounding. Parakka was here. Now it was up to him to deliver on his promise.

Since Gerdi had left him, Aurin had visited him several more times, to steal a kiss or to beg his forgiveness for the imminent destruction of Parakka. But as they talked, as she cried, as they kissed, there was one thing that lurked in his mind. He had to betray her, and it ate at his insides.

But he had made a promise, and he was compelled to keep it; and so he began preparations. He had been patient like never before. When the Princess was not with him, he spent every waking hour flexing his abilities, reaching out with his power and then drawing back just before he lost control. He had never been in an environment where there were so few distractions before, and if he allowed himself to lapse into thought he inevitably came back to his feelings about betraying Aurin; the pain of that was not something he relished dwelling on, so he did not allow himself to think at all. The combination of solitude and denial did wonders for his concentration.

So he practised, and practised, and practised. Gerdi had undone his Damper Collar so that he could put it on or take it off as necessary, and he always had a warning of anyone approaching his cell by the echoing footsteps in the corridor, giving him time to snap on the metal collar with the ice-white Damper Stone at his throat, leaving the tiny snap-catch loose. But visits were few and far between, and so he spent hours at a stretch just sitting on the floor of his cell, his brow furrowed in concentration, reaching out with his power, focusing, drawing back, and then reaching out further. If he overstepped himself just once, his spirit-stones would release the energy inside him, and the game would be up. He might destroy a section of the palace, but he would drain himself in doing so, and he would not be able to defend himself when they came to kill him.

Control. He had always been unable to rein in his power once it was unleashed. Like him, it was reckless. He had been getting better over time, but the progress was painfully slow.

Now everything relied on him keeping his head. If he lost control this time, then everything they had planned would be for nothing. Thousands of lives would be on his conscience.

The pressure was unbearable. But when the wind-siren started up, he knew that all the practice, all the preparation, everything had come down to this. This one moment, this infinitesimal pivot on which the fate of a world revolved.

On such small things are kingdoms built and destroyed, he thought; and then he stood up, closed his eyes, bowed his head and clenched his fist.

It was time.

He undid his Damper Collar. All Damper Stones gave off a charge that crippled the spirit-stones within their area of effect. With only a single Damper Stone, the aura was generally only enough to affect the person wearing it; for it to have even a minor influence on another person's spirit-stones, the wearer would have to be practically hugging him or her. However, the auras of Damper Stones were cumulative, in the same way as spirit-stones; that was, the more that were placed together, the more powerful they were and the greater their area of effect. When his energy had been sapped in Takami's bedchamber, there had been many piled together. With the single stone on his collar, he only had to hold it away from him and he was out of its range.

Freed, he felt the first surge of the Flow from his stones and checked it ruthlessly. Starting again, he let the energy trickle out, a warming glow that spread into his chest. Like a sheepdog driving a herd, he fought to keep the energy together, and reined it in when it sought to break out of his control. Slowly, he opened another floodgate inside, only the tiniest crack, giving the trapped energy an outlet, directing it along his arms and into his hands, shutting off the Flow from his stones so that all that was left were two small, throbbing pockets of energy that burned beneath the skin of his palm.

Then, with steps so measured and careful that he might have been balancing plates on his shoulders, he walked across the cell and placed his hand on the door. In his mind, the wind-siren was silent. The feel of the cell floor through his boots was gone. All there was was the lock, and the power in his hand. He placed his left palm on it, sweat inching its way down from his hairline.

It all comes down to this, he thought.

Now!

The surge of power was short and brutal, and he viciously shut it off a moment after it got loose. The lock blew outwards, its ivory substance smashing into splinters beneath his palm, and the door shuddered under the force.

He opened his eyes. The lock was destroyed. His second pocket of power waited in his right hand.

"*Yeah!*" he cried in exultation, throwing open the cell door and leaping out into the corridor. The Guardsman sentry – who had been stunned by the blast so close to him – raised his halberd to fire, but he was too slow. Ryushi stepped inside the range of his weapon, pressed his right palm to the Guardsman's metal chest and loosed the energy stored there. An explosion of concussion blasted his hair flat, and blew the Guardsman heavily into the curved creamstone wall of the corridor. The sentry collapsed, his halberd falling free.

"Yeah! Yeah, yeah, *yeah!*" Ryushi muttered to himself. "I got it at *last!*" He looked up and down the empty corridor, feeling the energy still stored in his spirit-stone battery, and smiled to himself.

"Phase Two," he said, and took hold of the Guardsman's wrists, dragging him into the cell, before returning to pick up the halberd and closing the door behind him.

The Keriags hit the palace with the fury of a tornado. The hastily assembled array of vehicles and war-machines that had sallied out of the bowels of Fane Aracq met the onslaught with crushing wheels and thumping salvos of force-cannon fire. Turrets and cupolas swivelled on the palace walls, hissing steam as they aligned and fired, blasting concussion bolts into the endless horde, scattering the black bodies of the Keriags. Parakkan wyverns engaged the Princess's Riders, screeching and swooping and wheeling as the Artillerists that rode shotgun traded fire. Keriags splintered and cracked beneath the great tracked wheels of Aurin's war-machines, while others swarmed up and over their metal bodies, hacking at them with their *gaer bolga*.

The battle was strangely weighted. On Aurin's side, there were precious few foot-troops – for she knew better than to send them out against Keriags – but plenty of immense, impenetrable vehicles that rumbled slowly around the battlefield, things of steam and weathered iron powered by their Pilots. On the side of Parakka, only those troops that could move fast enough to keep up with the Keriags had been brought: a fleet of wyverns and a group of pakpaks that were arriving at the rear. Aurin's forces were powerful but slow and few in number. Parakka's were fast and numerous, but they lacked the strength to do any real damage to the Princess's war-machines.

Hochi, Gerdi and Calica hung back on a single wyvern, soaring high in the twilight above the battle. Hochi was in the front of the harness, lying low against the creature's massive neck, his thick fingers steering them with the confidence of years of experience. They watched the fight below, their eyes flickering anxiously over the mayhem, and hoped that it was not all for nothing.

The Keriags were allowing themselves to be held back. They pushed up against the soaring palace walls, but they did not attempt to scale them. From what Calica had seen of the Keriags, even smooth, curved walls with no obvious grip would be little problem to the insectoid creatures. The war-machines could cut swathes through the ranks of black chitin, but they could not prevent the horde from swarming round them and up to the palace. The Keriags could storm Fane Aracq and gut it in less than a quarter-cycle. But they did not. They were waiting for the signal from the Queens. They would sense when the heartstone had been removed, by the reaction in the offspring stones set deep inside them. That would be the moment when they attacked. Until then, all they had to do was sow confusion, even at the expense of their own lives. But then, what was a Keriag but a single part of a whole, subservient to the needs of its hive? Their lives meant nothing, if the hive survived.

"Ryushi better know what he's doing in there," Gerdi commented, his eyes on the cloudlike palace that rose like a mountain amid the ocean of combatants.

"And what if he *gets* the stone?" Calica said sharply. She had been snappish ever since they had left Base Usido. "What if this stupid Splitling idea doesn't work? If Elani's wrong?"

"We can put the stone back on Aurin," Hochi said over his shoulder. "That'll stop the Keriags turning on us. However, that does mean that—"

"Ryushi doesn't *know* about our idea! He doesn't know to keep Aurin near by in case it goes wrong! What if he kills her?"

"Oh, I doubt that," said Gerdi, then realized who he was talking to and shut up.

Calica's shoulders tightened in a physical

reaction to the reminder Gerdi had just dealt her. More quietly she said: "What I mean is, there's still so much that can go wrong."

Gerdi turned his face into the wind and frowned. "No. He promised me that he'd look out for his friends first, before anything. If he takes that stone, he won't put it back on her. Even if the Keriags die, and she dies with them. 'Cause if he gives the stone back, then she's still got the Keriags, and we're all dead anyway."

"But what if—" Calica began.

"He *won't*, okay?" Gerdi said. "He promised me." Then, quieter, to himself: "He *promised* me."

* * *

"What are they *doing*?" Aurin cried, looking out of one of the oval wind-holes of her chambers.

+++ My lady, we should leave +++ Tatterdemalion buzzed from where he crouched by the enormous, ornate wall-mirror.

"Leave? Leave *where*?" she raged. "Where can I go? Running will solve nothing. Without the Keriags, I have no *power*. No, I must stay, at least until I know what has caused this sudden turn."

"The Parakkans are behind it, Princess," said Corm, standing by the door, the pale skin of his bald head made ghostly by the white glowstone near by. "All the more reason why we should leave now, while we can."

"No! We cannot weaken!" she shouted, her voice shrill with fear and anger. "The Keriags know that my death would mean their death. They know that my heartstone, if removed, will kill them all. That is the circle we are trapped in, yes?"

+++ It seems the Keriags intend to break that circle +++ Tatterdemalion observed.

"They must have a plan," Corm said, his Augmented eyes chattering as they moved from the Princess to the Jachyra and back again. "Isn't it a little coincidental that the Parakkans thought to pre-empt our strike on their headquarters? Perhaps the prisoner got a message away somehow. I would—"

"Impossible!" Aurin snapped. "And should you suggest again that any of this is *my* fault, Corm, I will have you executed! I know what you think of the way I have handled the prisoner! Didn't we find the hideout, *without* using the Scour?"

"Then why is he still *alive*?" Corm hissed.

+++ **This arguing is pointless** +++ Tatterdemalion said, his mechanical voice cutting in. +++ **We must act instead** +++

"What if running is what they *want* us to do, yes?" Aurin said, looking back out of the wind-hole. "What if we would just be falling into their trap?" She suddenly turned and fixed her gaze on Tatterdemalion. "What about the Keriags in the Dominions? Do they act in the same way? Does my *father* know of this?"

+++ **The Keriags in the Dominions seem unaffected by this uprising** +++ Tatterdemalion crackled. +++ **Though I have no doubt that they are aware of it. They are biding their time. The King is away on his survey of the southern deserts, and out of contact by normal means. He relies on my Jachyra to keep him in touch with events** +++

"Good. Then he can find out about this little . . . *incident* after it's over, yes?"

+++ **Understood, my lady** +++

She looked back out of the wind-hole at the raging battle below.

"Fetch me the prisoner," she said suddenly. "Corm, no arguments, do it now."

Corm hesitated for the slightest of moments, then bowed and left, his footsteps dying as the door closed behind him.

"What are they *doing*?" she whispered to herself again, her fingers running absently over the three turquoise stones that hung cold against her collarbone.

Ryushi swallowed, the acid taste of fear stinging the back of his mouth. He felt like he was not really there, that he was watching everything through a spyglass and that the events occurring around him were merely a play before his eyes, powerless to physically affect him. The corridors of Fane Aracq, and the people that hurried past him, were rendered in a greyer palette than the naked eye when seen through the eyepieces of a Guardsman's helmet. The black carapace of armour surrounded him, weighing heavily on his shoulders and legs and head, pressing and pinching uncomfortably in some places, so loose that it chafed in others. It was a bad fit, and there was a dent in the chest where he had loosed his power on the previous occupant, but it would have to do.

He headed for Aurin's chambers, his halberd clutched in both hands, jogging along as fast as he dared in the cumbersome armour. He was not used to the weight, and he did not trust himself not to trip if he ran too fast. Nobody stopped to give him more than a glance; the interior of Fane Aracq was in turmoil. Nobles shouted at each other in panic, retainers scurried back and forth to try and secure escape for their masters, Guardsmen hurried to different posts. The noise and chaos washed around the black metal of his armour, and muffled by his helmet, the boy inside was untouched.

Gerdi had supplied him with general directions to where he thought the Princess's chambers were, but it soon became obvious that they were painfully insufficient in the maze of corridors. In despair of ever finding Aurin on his own, he took a risk. Grabbing a Guardsman who was hurrying the other way, he hollered at him urgently.

"The Princess! Quick, where are the Princess's

chambers? I have an important message for the Princess!"

"Two levels up, and keep going in this direction," the Guardsman replied, equally urgently.

"My thanks!" Ryushi said, slapping him on the shoulder in a rough, companionable way, and hurried off.

"You'll need clearance!" the Guardsman shouted after him.

Ryushi raised one hand in acknowledgement, but he did not slow. He supposed that, in a place as big as this, it would not seem suspicious for the occasional person to ask directions; and in the confusion, the man would probably have not thought about it anyway before he made his reply.

He had just found the moulded creamstone steps that led up to the next level when he stopped, a judder of panic running through his body. There, descending the curved steps, was Corm, the loyal Machinist that Aurin kept as her aide. Could his mechanical eyes see through Ryushi's improvized disguise? Would he recognize the Damper Collar at his Guardsman's utility belt for what it was? Conscious that his pause would make him look suspicious, he hurried onward, up the stairs. The chittering goggles of Corm's eyes seemed to bore into him as he approached, but then the moment was gone, and they passed each other on the wide stairwell. Ryushi jogged on, his heart pounding in his chest as if it would smash his ribs to splinters, his breathing loud in his ears inside his helmet.

Keep focused. Do what you have to. Everything relies on you.

The thought helped to drive him onward, to keep putting one foot in front of the other in the face of his mounting terror. He ascended another level and then ran out into a new corridor.

This one was different. At first, he was puzzled as to what the change was; but a moment later he realized. There were no torches here, no smokeless wychwood. White glowstones were set in the walls, making the light brighter and subtly different, without the yellow-orange tint of flame.

White glowstones? He was on the right track. It had to be close now.

Following the corridor, his heart lost some of its

buoyancy as he saw what was at the end of it. Three Guardsmen, standing before an ivory, carven door. This must be one of the security points that Gerdi had told him about. He had been lucky so far, in that most of them had been abandoned to stop them hindering the Guardsmen in defence of the palace. After all, it would be impossible to stop and check each person in the chaos, and it would make moving from one section of the palace to another an incredibly slow process. But the most important of them were still maintained, and this was one. The Princess's chambers lay within, of that he was sure.

He walked steadily down the long, tubelike corridor towards them, and the sentries looked up at him, expecting him to state his business. But inside his armour, the quiet hum of his spirit-stones was building.

"Nothing's happening!" Calica cried, looking over Gerdi's shoulder at the battle below. "Why don't they attack?"

Gerdi followed her gaze. From their vantage point, high up on wyvern-back, the battlefield was an endless, swarming mass of black – the Keriags' numbers seemed inexhaustible – through which the occasional hulking shape of a war-machine lumbered, sowing concussion-bolts to all sides. Some of the war-machines had been taken out, either by a choice shot from one of the dogfighting wyverns, or because their tracks and wheels were so choked with the tough bodies of the crushed Keriags that they could not move any longer. The Princess's fleet of Riders still attacked from the purple skies, and the palace guns were still fully operational, their heavy *whoomph* audible even at this distance. But still the Keriags would not assault Fane Aracq, staying outside the walls where they were being slowly but steadily massacred.

"Ryushi hasn't got the necklace yet," said Gerdi. "Gotta give him time."

"We don't *have* time! Right now Takami's probably already at Base Usido. Every minute we waste here means—"

"Hey, I *know* what it means, alright?" Gerdi snapped over his shoulder. "We've got to give him *time!*"

7

The Twisting, Stabbing Stain

The forces of Maar hit Base Usido like a sledgehammer.

Reports had been that the army had entered the Rifts two cycles beforehand, but after that the scouts had lost them. Parakka no longer had the manpower to send troops into the Rifts to harass the army on their way; for without sufficient skill and numbers, they would most likely be killed by the angry beasts that roamed the near forests, still smarting from their recent defeat. The few wyverns they had left they dared not use to keep an eye on the army in case Takami's own wyverns spotted them and shot them down. All they could do was dig in and wait, and hope that the hostile terrain of the Rifts would keep Takami's army out as efficiently as it kept the Parakkans in.

The first strike came out of nowhere. Skimming dangerously low over the treetops of the Rifts, a fleet of twelve wyverns heralded the arrival of Takami, and the end of that frail hope. They came from the west, not from the north-east like the rest of the army, plunging down the cliff faces into the huge, flat valley where Base Usido lay and screaming across the twilight plains. Their Riders arced them into a wide turn, the green-armoured Artillerists on their backs spraying the settlement with concussion bolts as they banked. Huts exploded into splinters, sending a deadly rain of spikes that thudded into everything and everyone near by. The cliff-face lifts that linked the main body of the base to the clifftop defences took a pounding; huge chunks of rubble and heavy, snaking metal cables crashed down on to the structures below. Force-bolts raked the wyvern hatchery, reducing its already damaged shell to a mass of crumpled metal. People ran shouting and screaming, women hurrying their children indoors, fighters running to the defence of their base, all amid the shattering bolts of force that rained down on them like meteors, destroying everything they hit.

Their first pass complete, the wyverns turned, their bellies skimming the cliff face as they banked to race back along the plain, ready to turn and fire again.

That was when the counterstrike hit. Two wyverns were blasted from the sky, their bodies pulverized, before any of the Riders realized what was happening. Before they had located where the attack was coming from, three more were sent spinning to the ground, their force-cannons imploding with a flat *whoomph* on impact.

They had expected a few wyverns, at most. Instead, what they saw was mukhili. Three of them, the gargantuan beetle-like creatures from the southern deserts of the Dominions, lumbering out from the caves at the base of the cliffs. And strapped to each of their immense carapaces were not just one but four force-cannons, each one mounted on a pivot and firing independently of the others, setting up a close mesh of near-constant fire. The dark-skinned desert-folk that rode in howdahs on their backs whooped and jeered as the Parakkan Artillerists zeroed in on another wyvern, three bolts from the same mukhili hitting it simultaneously and annihilating it.

And then the Parakkan wyverns joined the fray, those few that had been left behind in defence of the Base, launching themselves from their hiding places on the surrounding cliffs and soaring down towards the intruders. Takami's wyverns were caught in a sudden crossfire, and two more of them fell before they retreated back to where they had come from, their numbers decimated by two-thirds.

But their assault had been planned to coincide with the arrival of the ground forces, and their timing was good. No sooner had the noise of the first attack died down than the forest around Base Usido's clifftop defences erupted in a hail of force-cannon fire, as the first of the foot troops arrived. The air warped and swelled around the invisible bolts of energy as they flew back and forth, smashing trees or denting the spiked outer wall. The Guardsmen's halberds were less powerful than the force-cannons operated by

Parakkan Artillerists, but they were far more numerous, and each blast punched the wall with enough force to bend it inwards. Enough hits and it would fall.

"They're staying back in the trees!" Jaan shouted in Peliqua's ear over the noise. They were standing just inside the perimeter, surrounded by the yells and hollering of the Artillerists and the other fighters as they ran to and fro, co-ordinating attacks and carrying orders. High above them, the turret-mounted force-cannons hissed and spat steam as they swivelled, recoiling violently with each devastating blast.

"They don't want to risk a full-on attack!" Peliqua shouted back.

((Perhaps the trek through the Rifts has decimated them more than they wish to let on)) Iriqi observed through a bright fog of mingled hope and alarm. The Koth Taraan, like its companions, could not help in the defence of the wall as it possessed no weapon that could reach the enemy; instead, they waited anxiously, ready to react to a breach or to be called elsewhere in the Base.

"If they had waited for the whole of Aurin's army, they could have swept through the Rifts with no problem at all," Peliqua said. "It's this horrible, horrible place. You need the strength of numbers, or few enough people so you can be stealthy. But Takami's awful mad, and he wants to get in first. Oh! I wonder how Kia feels about all this?"

"All I'm hoping is that they had to leave most of their heavy equipment behind," said Jaan gravely. He talked a lot more nowadays, since his friendship with the Koth Taraan had brought him out of his shell a little. "See, the Rifts are hard to get *out* of at short notice – that's why we couldn't evacuate everyone – but it's just as hard to get *into*," he said, explaining for Iriqi's benefit. "With the way the ground drops sheer in some places, you can't get war-machines up or down the cliffs without a lot of manpower and machinery to help you out. And if you don't know the Rifts like we do, it can be made twice as hard." He paused, his yellow eyes feral. "That's why Aurin was taking so long to assemble her people. Takami's haste might be our best chance for survival."

* * *

On the lower plain, the Guardsmen were arriving, abseiling down the vast cliffs, hundreds of tiny threads supporting minuscule soldiers against the immensity of the rock. Bereft of their air support, they were proving to be easy targets for the Artillerists on the backs of the mukhili, who picked them off as they descended; but they had the advantage of numbers, and their descent was fast, and they were artfully spread so as not to allow the cannons to take out more than one at a time. Soon the base of the cliffs was thick with Guardsmen, and the mukhili had to concentrate on defending themselves rather than attacking the abseiling troops.

At that moment, both sides threw in another card from their hands. The wyverns that had been repulsed in the first strike reappeared, this time bringing with them more of Takami's fleet, swooping low over the valley to deliver a few cursory blasts at the mukhili before sending another shattering salvo into the Base, smashing buildings and people alike with their concussion bolts. And at the same time, the gates of Base Usido opened and out poured what was left of the

Parakkan troops, riding on horse or pakpak, charging across the plains towards the enemy. With them came cricktracks – converted for war with crude force-cannons and blades – and an assortment of other haulage vehicles, each one brimming with troops.

Last came the giant construction machine nicknamed the Mule, a huge crane that ran on two massive, triangular sets of treads. Its arm was a towering thing of weather-beaten iron, riding on a flat, squarish base, with a massive hook at its tip. It had been one of the first machines that had been made during the erection of Base Usido, and the one that had borne most of the brunt of the heavy loads that followed: the building of the hatchery and the stables, the assembly of the perimeter walls, lifting of force-cannons and so on. But now it had a new use, as an engine of war; its flat body was the perfect platform for force-weapons, and warriors crowded on its back with shoulder-mounted cannons as it rumbled out of the gates of Base Usido. At the helm, hidden behind thick iron plating, one boy's knuckles gripped the control levers tightly, his spirit-stones burning with energy, forcing life into the veins of the awesome machine. Ty, the Pilot.

Kia was there, too, riding on the back of the Mule, crouched low with one hand gripping the handle of the Pilot's hatch for support, the other holding her bo staff close. She cried out in exultation as they thundered into the fray, the old hate back in her eyes again, the cold fire that burned at the thought of killing those who served Macaan. Her thirst for revenge was an unknown quantity, and nobody – least of all Kia herself – knew the depths that her well of rage went to. But here, in the heat of impending battle, it was clear that there was a way to go yet before it ran dry.

The two fronts collided, their disorderly advance troops pouring into each other with unstoppable momentum. The sound of concussion-bolts and the dull rumble of thousands of armoured feet were drowned out by the clash of hand-to-hand combat as the fighters joined weapons savagely. Parakkans slid off the backs of the slow-moving construction machines, throwing themselves into battle; and within minutes the two sides had met and merged into one great mass, and the plains were alive with combat.

Kia had meant to stay on the back of the Mule with the others that remained to guard it, their bows thudding and cannons thumping as they fired from the raised platform. She had meant to stay near Ty, to help keep away the Guardsmen that tried to clamber on to the slow-moving metal beast. But the battle fired her blood with iceburn, and she lost all thought of tactics or strategy in the rush. Screaming her hate, she flung herself headlong into the fight, her staff cracking down on the shoulder of a Guardsman as she leaped down from the back of the Mule, and lost herself in the twisting, stabbing stain that spread across the blue grass of the plains.

Back at the clifftop defences, the fortunes of Parakka were ailing. The stalemate was rapidly coming to an end now, and only one conclusion was likely. The towering metal wall of spikes that circumscribed the compound had buckled and broken in several places, great plates of iron torn from their rivets and hanging inward under the hammering barrage of force-bolts from the Guardsmen that hid in the treeline. The near edge of the forest was a shattered mess of splinters now, a thick haze of sawdust hanging in the air amid the fallen boughs of the haaka trees, and the bodies of Guardsmen lay scattered all around. Five of them had fallen to every one Parakkan, but they had been relentless, their armoured forms darting from cover to cover as they kept up their ceaseless assault. And it was paying off at last. The wall was about to break.

"Get ready for it!" somebody shouted above the noise.

But there was one thing to give them hope. Takami had been forced to sacrifice many troops during his assault. It would have been unnecessary to use that many men had he managed to get even *one* mobile force-cannon to the Base, of a size such as the ones that defended Fane Aracq. But, as Jaan had hoped, Takami had been unable to get his heavy machinery across the terrain of the Rifts with the limited resources of his relatively small army, and so he had been forced to rely on this costly use of men to gradually batter down the walls of Base Usido with their smaller force-cannon halberds.

Takami had many soldiers, and they were well armoured and well equipped; but he had been forced to strip his army down to the bare essentials on his journey across the Rifts, and had endured many attacks on the way by the rampaging Rift-beasts. Parakka were in with a chance, more of a chance than any of them had dared to believe.

Unless Takami had something else up his sleeve.

At that moment, the wall came down. A final, concerted blast ripped out from the dark treeline, and a great section of the perimeter wall groaned and toppled inward, tearing away from its neighbours and buckling them backwards in the process. The defenders that manned the ledge that ran around the inside of the wall howled in alarm as they fell, some to be crushed underneath the falling plate of metal, some to scramble to safety.

Jaan felt the sinking nausea of the inevitable

conflict in his belly, even before he heard the wind-siren suddenly screech out from the forest. The signal for attack. All around him, Parakkans were rushing towards the breach to plug it, but the Guardsmen were already breaking from cover, surging through the rain of concussion bolts towards the gap they had created. He swallowed bile, and looked to his right, his yellow eyes meeting the cream-on-white of his sister's.

"Ready?" she asked, all flightiness gone from her.

He nodded slowly; and then, as one, the Kirin girl and the halfbreed ran into the combat, followed by the awesome bulk of the Koth Taraan.

Jaan clashed his forearms together as the throng of black-armoured Guardsmen rose up to meet them, his dagnas slicing out of their wooden tubes in response. Next to him, Peliqua's manriki-gusari snaked around her like something alive, the deadly lead weights at each end spinning in a twilight blur. She glanced at her brother once; but if she had had any doubts before about his ability to handle himself, she lost them then. She was his elder sister, and she had always set herself up as his protector, shielding him from the prejudices and troubles that his halfbreed blood brought him; but now she saw that he needed no protection from her any more. She had not been there to save him in the caves during the Bane attack, and he had come through that just fine.

But she was still his sister, and they were still a team; and as they entered the battle, their movements were so fluidly synchronized that they seemed to share the same mind. Her chain lashed around the wrist of a Guardsman, yanking him forward and into the driving path of Jaan's dagnas, while the other end spun over her brother's head as he ducked, smashing brutally into the faceplate of another Guardsman who was aiming a swipe at him. A moment later, Jaan was parrying for her while she loosed her chain from the dead Guardsman's wrist and wrapped it around the second Guardsman's throat, cracking his neck. The two moved as one, sweat flying free from their faces as they tackled the invaders, trying to hold them out.

But they would not be held out.

The Guardsmen's superior armour and weight lent them the advantage in the press of the breach, and they were steadily applying their efforts to forcing the Parakkans back from the gap, pushing their way in as they hacked and sliced with the bladed edges of their halberds. Nobody saw what their real intention was at first; everybody's mind was on the fight that surrounded them. But when the Guardsmen had pushed far enough inside, the Parakkans saw suddenly the mistake they had made. They weren't trying to power their way inside; they were only trying to secure the sides of the breach so they could get up the inside of the wall. The black-armoured figures poured in, clambering up the ladders to where the force-cannon turrets were, overpowering the few guards that had been left there. And before the Parakkans could stop them, they had loosed their halberds on the Artillerists that powered the cannons, compact blasts of force that pulverized the operators and left them limp and dead.

But worse was yet to come. The sudden silencing of the Parakkan guns heralded a second wave of Guardsmen who had been hanging far back in the forest. Now with nothing to fear from the wall defences, they boldly ran across the shattered and cratered battlefield and began to blast at the edges of the breach, concentrating their fire on the seams of the wall. In moments, another section of the wall leaned inwards and then collapsed, and this time it brought its neighbour down with it. The breach had been torn open too wide to plug now, and the Guardsmen swarmed in with redoubled fury.

The fray resounded with the shrieks of the wounded and the trampled, the hum and release of spirit-stones and the muted thumps of the Guardsmen's halberds as they loosed their concussion-bolts. Through it all, Iriqi stood by Jaan and Peliqua, its outsize claws rending and swatting the enemy like they were toys, tearing through armour and limbs with equal ease. The Koth Taraan rose like a blood-spattered mountain in the midst of the combat. Force-bolts only rocked it, but did no real damage. The blades of the halberds were ineffective. It was as the rock it resembled; immovable, unstoppable.

And then Peliqua's eyes fell on what was happening in the rear ranks of the Guardsmen, and she cried out in warning; but there was nothing anyone could do now to prevent what was about to occur. For amid the beetle-black of the Guardsmen were the green-armoured figures of Artillerists, Takami's Artillerists this time, and they were ascending the ladders with heavy escorts to where the vacant force-cannon turrets waited. She realized then what was about to happen, and grabbed Jaan's upper arm.

"Get back! We've gotta get out of here!"

Jaan responded immediately, trusting her without question. They began to fall back as fast as they could, Peliqua shouting her warning to anyone who would listen, Iriqi moving with them. Some heeded her, joining the fighting retreat towards the cliff top. Most stood their ground.

That was when the force-cannons began firing again.

Takami's Artillerists had taken over the steam-driven swivel turrets, and now the great guns pointed not outwards but inwards, directed down at the Parakkan forces. Suddenly, the tables were turned, and it was not the Guardsmen who faced the barrage of force-bolts but the defenders. Inevitably, some of the front ranks of black-armoured fighters were caught in the ensuing destruction; but mostly the semi-invisible ripples crashed over their heads and into the Parakkans, throwing them violently through the air or smashing them where they stood. The onslaught was more than the beleaguered fighters could take, and the last of their resistance crumbled under the shattering force of the assault. The defence dissolved into a rout, as the Parakkans ran for their lives.

But they were on the top edge of a cliff, with a drop of several hundred feet behind them. There was nowhere to go.

"Come on! Get in!" Peliqua yelled, ushering a young, wounded Kirin man into the lift with her. There were ten in the metal cage of the lift now, including Iriqi, who took up the space of four. Already she could feel the groaning of the protesting supports, and she glanced doubtfully at the huge Koth Taraan and hoped that the lift would take its weight. She pulled the barrier closed behind the wounded man, sandwiching him inside the close press of the lift, and then yanked the lever downward to descend.

Only those that had heeded Peliqua's warning – and others who had seen what she had seen and reacted in time – had got the head-start necessary to get to the lifts on the cliff edge. The retreating Parakkans were being hacked down near by, caught between the halberds of the Guardsmen and the blasts of the force-cannons. Peliqua could feel the shock of each impact stirring her red braids against her ash-grey skin. But now she looked down at the terrible damage that Takami's first strike – the wyvern assault – had wreaked on the cables, chains, winches and pulleys that ran all the way up the cliff face, and she hoped that the lift she had chosen was one that would work. Already, the other lifts were full; and some were not moving at all, or had halted a little way down, marooning their occupants.

The second's delay that she knew would occur between her pulling the lever and the lift starting to move seemed endless, stretching out for longer than a second could possibly last. . .

And then, with a lurch, the lift jolted and began to grind its way down the sheer cliff towards the ground below, mercifully carrying the sights and sounds of the massacre above them further and further away as they descended.

Kia rammed her staff hard into the ground, and the earth rose up in a thick ripple that spread out in a semicircle from where she stood, bulging beneath the feet of the Guardsmen that faced her and throwing them to the ground. The less battle-weary of the Parakkans took ruthless advantage, jumping on their fallen opponents and running them through, while their exhausted or wounded companions used the respite to pull back from the front ranks. Next to them, the immense presence of the Mule rumbled onwards, driving the enemy before it, cracking the bones of the dead under its treads.

The Parakkan troops on the plain, unaware that their Base had already been invaded, were faring better than their companions who guarded the clifftop defences. Takami's troops had been unable to get any machinery or even any pakpaks down on to the plains, for the Parakkans had brought all the cargo lifts to the valley floor and guarded them heavily as soon as they knew of Takami's imminent arrival. In contrast, the Parakkans had both an abundance of pakpaks and a good many vehicles, crude though they were. Despite being outnumbered, they held the upper hand, and exploited it without remorse.

Many of the troops had rallied around the twin foci of Kia and Ty, and were forming a tight offensive knot that the enemy were finding hard to keep back. Kia's battle savagery was legendary among Parakkans since the Integration, and now she found herself once more a leader as she threw herself body and soul into the fight. Her shouted orders were followed eagerly, for she had trained herself well in tactics, and despite her inner fury she kept her reason on a tight rein. If she had been able to see herself, she might have thought how similar she had become to Calica now: both of them tacticians and leaders, forged by war; both of them orphaned by Macaan; both of them with a fierce love for Ryushi, though the nature of it was different. Had circumstances been otherwise, they should have been friends and allies instead of rivals. But the last link was not there, the bond that might have hung between them, and in its place was a bitter enmity.

With her was Ty, whose selfless sacrifice during that same battle had earned him the respect of his contemporaries. The crane arm of the Mule served as a beacon to the troops, stabbing high out of the fray, and the rumbling presence of the mobile fortress of grease and iron was the point from which Kia launched her many attacks. Elsewhere, the lumbering mukhili cut swathes into Takami's forces, the batteries of force-cannons on their backs sending pulses of concussion into the Guardsmen, while their vast mandibles swept up clusters of the hapless enemy and bit them in two.

It seemed that the Guardsmen had no defence against the strength of Parakka's most formidable weapons. But it was a false sense of security. For in the sky, the last of the Parakkan wyverns was dropping in a ragged spiral, its bones shattered; and the three remaining Riders in Takami's fleet turned their red-visored faces to the battle below, and saw what was happening there. They signalled to each other, unnoticed above the combatants, and then they acted.

The gunners on the backs of the mukhili had forgotten about shooting down the wyverns overhead since the ground engagement had begun. The Parakkan riders had been keeping Takami's wyverns occupied, dogfighting beneath the twilit eye of the Kirin Taq sun. But now the Parakkans were gone, and the victors were free to fire at whatever they chose. But it was not the mukhili that the Riders flew towards, with the Artillerists in the harnesses behind them sighting their cannons with deadly aim. It was the Mule. They saw how the troops clustered around it, using it as an impenetrable island from which to stage their forays; and they intended to take it out.

Kia heard the shriek of one of the wyverns as it powered downwards, a thin challenge above the chaos of the combat, and she took a step back from the fight, brushed her red hair away from her forehead and looked up. Her pupils shrank in terror as she saw –

The three force-bolts tore into the Mule simultaneously, rending through the metal and blasting it into ragged leaves of shrapnel that peppered the surrounding Parakkans with deadly flying blades. One of the huge, triangular tracks was blown free of the main body, tipping over sideways and crushing those below it. The crane arm had half of its supports destroyed; and like a tree chopped by a woodcutter, it toppled sideways with a monolithic howl of tortured iron and fell on to the fray below, killing Guardsman and Parakkan alike. The flat body of the Mule also took a direct hit, cracking it in half, the shockwave sending those on its back writhing through the air.

In the space of a few seconds, what had been the largest construction machine in the Parakkan force had been reduced to a broken, derelict cripple, slumped at an angle amid the blood and smashed bodies of those it had fallen on.

"*Ty!*" Kia screamed, all battle-fury gone now, dissipating in the face of the clawed grip of terror that seized her. Ignoring the fight around her – which had continued without a pause – she pushed her way back through the troops that had adopted her as a leader. She did not notice their expectant glances, or the way that they looked to her to provide a new game-plan now that the Mule was defunct. She was focused on only one thing: Ty.

I'll not lose you again, she swore.

She reached the immense form of the shattered thing, shoved her bo staff into the crossbelts on her back and began to climb. The dented and makeshift surface of the Mule's outer armour provided easy handholds for her, and she clambered up to the struts of the undamaged tracks with the thoughtless skill of the mountain-born, one who had been climbing since she could walk. From there she pulled herself up to the flat roof, which now listed at a treacherous downward angle, and slid down the decline towards the Pilot's hatch, skirting the edge of the jagged rent of twisted metal where the Mule's body had split in half. Around the broken vehicle, the battle continued to rage, the Guardsmen being steadily beaten away. Her heart was thumping against her ribs as she grasped the handle of the Pilot's hatch, and her breathing came hard.

This happened before, she thought, the words flashing through her head with diamond clarity. *First we're forced into an attack against Fane Aracq, just like the Ley Warren last time. And now Ty's down and I'm here to pull him out, just like in the Bear Claw. Is this what war is? Is history just gonna repeat itself until there's nobody left to record it any more? Is there any point to it at all?*

But what if this time the results are different? What if this time we win at Fane Aracq? What if Ty –?

She twisted the handle and pulled the hatch open, dread flooding through her. The cockpit had been built for one, and it was close and dark, with a faded orange glowstone lighting the banks of brass levers and palm-studs and steam-releases. Ty was there, his shoulders limp, his head back and his mouth open, his unruly black hair falling down his neck.

"*Ty!*" she cried, reaching in and shaking him. He jolted, and a long groan escaped his lips, but his eyes did not open. A broad smile of desperate relief spread across Kia's face at the sound he made, but it did not last long. He could be badly hurt, and she could not afford to leave him here. Not her Ty. She withdrew herself, kneeling up and looking around. A tall, broad-shouldered Kirin man with a white mohawk was getting to his feet on the ground near by, stunned but unharmed amid the wreckage of the Mule. It took her only a moment to recognize him.

"Aaris! I need some help here!" she shouted.

The Kirin looked around, saw her, and seemed to shake off his daze. He clambered up the slope of the Mule's body to reach her, and between them they managed to manhandle Ty out of the cockpit and down to the ground.

"Find me a pakpak," she ordered harshly, all courtesy lost in the concern for her loved one. Aaris understood, though, and he was quick to comply. Kia ran her hands over Ty, checking him for broken bones, her face taut with worry; but he appeared unharmed apart from a lump at the base of his skull where he had hit his head. She patted his cheek, talking to him, trying to wake him, and was rewarded with a slight lifting of his lids. The

157

pupils beneath were unfocused and ranged wildly around, but he was at least partially awake. She smiled again, her battle-bloodied features shining from within at the sight.

"Don't you ever leave me," she said, the words hardly audible over the noise of the nearby combat and the sounds of the mukhili's cannon batteries obliterating the last of Takami's wyverns.

And then Aaris was there, pushing back through the throng of Parakkans, leading an alarmed pakpak by its reins. Between them, Kia and Aaris helped Ty into the saddle, and she swung herself up behind him. The pakpak lowed in protest, accustomed to only one rider at a time, but Kia ignored it. This was war; everyone had to carry more than their share of the burden.

Kia's eyes met Aaris's, still holding the reins, and between the Dominion girl and the Kirin there passed unspoken thanks; then Kia spurred her mount, heading back through the fields of the fallen towards Base Usido, and Aaris picked up a double-bladed axe and returned to the fray.

8

Daggers in a Spray

Aurin and Tatterdemalion looked up at the door together, suddenly alert.

"What was that?" Aurin demanded, her colour high.

The dull crack in the corridor outside had been heard by both of them, sounding like several sledgehammers hitting the creamstone wall in unison. A force-cannon bolt? But had it been fired from one of the Parakkan wyverns that swooped around the spires of Fane Aracq, or had it come from inside?

+++ I will investigate, my lady +++

"No," she said, taking a step away from the door. "Stay here. I may need you."

+++ As you wish +++ the Jachyra replied,

stepping closer to her, a ragged scarecrow of a bodyguard.

"Could someone have got into the palace?" she asked.

+++ There would not have been time to— +++ Tatterdemalion began to reply, but his buzzing voice was shredded by a sudden shock of concussion as the door blew inwards, sprinkling sharp chips of ivory and stone in amid the clatter as it fell to the floor. Aurin shrieked as she fell, borne down by her Chief of Jachyra as he pounced on her, protecting her with his body.

A Guardsman was there, the black, beetle-like figure standing amid the settling cloud of dust, his halberd discarded, the raw hum of Flow energy resonating from his body.

"Aurin! It's time to end this!" Ryushi roared through the speaking-grille of his mask.

Tatterdemalion moved like a blur, springing sideways off the prone form of the Princess and changing direction as he hit the floor, leaping forward at Ryushi, his retractable finger-claws flicking out with a sharp ring. But Ryushi was ready for him, and he threw out his hand, five rippling shards of energy shooting out like daggers in a spray. Two of them caught the Jachyra in mid-air, tossing him one way and then the other in rapid succession before sending him crashing in a sprawl to the floor at the base of the great wall-mirror.

"Ryushi! What are you *doing*?" Aurin cried, from where she lay.

But Tatterdemalion was already back on his feet, his scrawny, disproportionate body weaving insidiously, searching for an opening where he could strike again. Ryushi watched him intently through the eyepieces of his mask. He desperately wanted to get out of the restrictive Guardsman armour, to fight freely, but there had simply been no time. He had to keep the Jachyra away from him, but he dared not risk too much of his power in one blast in case it ran out of control.

+++ It seems Corm was right about this one +++ Tatterdemalion crackled, ending in a trailing squeal of feedback.

"No! Ryushi, how *could* you?" Aurin shrieked, getting to her feet, tears of anger and betrayal starting to her eyes.

Ryushi felt his throat tighten involuntarily at the sound of the grief in her voice, but he dared not look at her. Tatterdemalion was prowling towards him like a wildcat, waiting for him to make the next move. The creature was quick; he might be able to dodge anything Ryushi threw at him, now that he was ready for it. And if he did, Ryushi wouldn't have time for a follow-up strike before the Jachyra reached him.

In that moment, it came to him. He remembered with sudden clarity his first encounter with a Jachyra, back at Osaka Stud, when it had been after Elani. And how it had reacted when. . .

He dug the toe of his boot under a small chunk of rubble, one of many that were scattered around the chamber in the wake of his explosive entrance. Tatterdemalion saw the movement, his telescopic eye whirring as he looked down at Ryushi's foot. And then Ryushi kicked it, scooping it up with his foot and flinging it with as much force as he could.

The Jachyra sidestepped it neatly, almost casually, as it flew by. But it had not been

Tatterdemalion that Ryushi was aiming for. It was the wall-mirror behind him; and being the size it was, it was a target that was hard to miss. The chunk of rubble hit the edge of the mirror and shattered it, sending a wide, black spider-web of cracks across a quarter of its surface with a terse crunch. Tatterdemalion made an odd *wheep* of alarm, turning back to look over his shoulder as an instinctive reaction, to check that his escape route was still viable.

And Ryushi struck.

There had been no time to prepare the blow. It came directly from the batteries of his spirit-stones, channelled through his fists; one fast moment of release and then he clamped off the floodgates. A short, heavy double-punch of concentrated power, streaking an invisible line, forcing the slower air aside like water. It smashed into Tatterdemalion, blasting him backwards, his disjointed limbs flailing. He was thrown with sickening force into the mirror, cracking it further along its length, and then crumpled to the floor in a ragged, limp heap of belts and claws and scraps of cloth.

"*Stop* it!" Aurin screamed at him, and the elation of his victory suddenly faded. He pulled off his helmet, throwing it aside, and turned to her with his blond tentacles of hair falling free around his face. She was crying, her beauty marred by the flush of her tears. "What are you *doing*? Is this how much it all meant to you? That you come to try and *kill* me, yes?"

"It's the heartstone I want," Ryushi said, keeping his voice rigid because the sight of her in such distress was making his insides twist around on themselves.

"That *is* killing me!" she cried. "Don't you see?"

"I won't let them get to you," Ryushi said gravely.

"You can't stop them! The Keriags! They'll tear me to pieces!"

"There's. . ." Ryushi began. His throat tightened again suddenly, but he swallowed and started again. "There's thousands of lives at stake, Aurin. Thousands. I can't let you win." For a moment they faced each other across the once-beautiful room that was now scattered with rubble. "Give up the heartstone, Aurin. It's a curse that binds you to your father's will. You're not a tyrant by nature. You're not this callous and cruel because you want to be. You just don't know any *better*. You can free yourself if you—"

"Don't patronize me!" she shrieked. "I am the daughter of a line of kings that has ruled this land for generations! Who are you to tell me how I should and shouldn't be? To force your peasant views on a Princess? I *loved* you, Ryushi, despite everything that you were." She lowered her head, and when she raised it again, her eyes were suddenly dark. "But now I have to kill you."

She raised her slim hands, and they seethed and boiled with the green and black radiance that he had felt before, the terrible, unknown power that she wielded. His heart lurched at the sight, his body remembering the time when her angry touch had once brushed him with that power and made him tremble. A shadow seemed to wrap itself around her now, her beautiful features turned icy and merciless.

"It doesn't have to be like this, Aurin," Ryushi said, feeling the power charge up in his own stones. "Give me the heartstone. You can get away. The Keriags won't follow you; not if I have the stone."

"Lose everything? For you, yes? Because you think your Parakkan ideals are the way the world should be, you want me to give up *everything* and *everyone* I've ever *known*?" She laughed bitterly, advancing towards him with slow, deliberate steps. "Did you really imagine I would agree to your generous proposition, Ryushi? You *are* naïve."

"Aurin, I don't want to fight you."

"But Ryushi, *I* want to fight *you*. You've betrayed me, peasant. You hurt me."

"You knew what I was when you met me. You knew where my loyalties lay. I had no choice."

"And because of what you have done, nor now do I," Aurin said.

"Don't make me—" he began, but Aurin cut him off with a sharp laugh.

"Make you what? Use your power? Please try, Ryushi; you'll find it an educating experience."

And as she said it, she kept advancing, so close now that she might almost touch him; and he thought of his promise and unleashed the Flow.

It was like throwing water at a wall. Her defences were staggering. Such *power* she held, such complex weaves of bluff and decoy and raw impenetrable energy. The concussion blasted across the room, scattering the rubble anew and stirring the curled form of the Jachyra in the corner; but not a hair on Aurin's head was touched by the force.

She stood before him, a soft, mocking smile on her perfect lips, gazing at him in cruel amusement. Open-mouthed, speechless, he staggered back a step; for in assaulting the fortress of her power, he had finally determined the nature of it. Entropy. Chaos. The lack of pattern or organization. With her ability, she could turn order into disorder, make the bonds and structures that hold an object together collapse and decay and disintegrate. Her powers of destruction made his and Kia's seem pale and feeble in comparison, and the sheer *magnitude* of her energy awed him.

He could not beat her. He could not hope to.

"Now you see," she said, standing before him, her voice a whisper. "The world is a cruel place, Ryushi, and those with the highest ideals are not always the victors. But soon that won't worry you any more."

"I loved you, Aurin," Ryushi said suddenly. "And I still do. You have to know that, before I die."

Aurin's eyes welled with tears again, the raw fury in them softened suddenly. She kissed him then, and the kiss had all the tenderness and passion of a final parting. She embraced him, her slender arms wrapping around his body, the power in her held back just beneath her skin; and he returned the embrace and the kiss, his hand sliding up her back towards her hair as if for a last touch of her dark coils before the end.

And then he pulled away from her, and there was a sharp *click*, and the Damper Collar was around her throat.

"*No!*" she shrieked, her eyes full of horror as she realized that he had tricked her. As he had embraced her, he had taken the Collar from his belt and snapped it on her from behind. It was a crude job, trapping most of her hair beneath the tight band of metal, but it didn't matter. The lock was in place, the white Damper stone rested next to her skin, and her power was suddenly rendered impotent.

"Princess!" came a cry from the ruined doorway, and Ryushi gathered Aurin's neck in the crook of his arm and roughly pulled her away as Corm appeared. "Princess, what is—"

He fell silent as he saw what had occurred. Tatterdemalion, crumpled in a corner next to the shattered mirror but now beginning to move slightly as he regained consciousness; the room in turmoil, ornaments shattered and splinters of creamstone everywhere; and the prisoner, dressed in the uniform of a Guardsman, with his arm around the Princess's neck. Her eyes were pleading, panicky; she was genuinely in fear of her life, as she had never been before. His Augmented eyes spotted the edge of a Damper Collar on her throat. With that one glance, he understood everything, reconstructed exactly what had happened.

For a moment, he did not speak, just stood impassive behind the high wall of his collar, his metal claw-arm flexing and unflexing with a tiny whirr. Then: "Let her go."

"Take a step closer, and I'll kill her. Look around you. You can see what my power does. You know I can do it," Ryushi said, his voice devoid of emotion.

"The Damper stone; you're too close," Corm said. "Your own stones will be affected."

"You sure? That's a chance you want to take?"

Corm hesitated. "Let her go *now*," he repeated, a waver of near-panic in his voice as his flimsy façade of control began to crumble.

Ryushi reached around her, his hand clamping around the largest of the turquoise stones that hung against Aurin's slender collarbone, and tore her necklace from her, the silver chain snapping free against her nape. Aurin gave a shriek of such pain and animal terror that Ryushi shuddered; but he gritted his teeth, and held her head brutally still, and she subsided into sobbing. He raised the heartstone high above his head, showing it to Corm.

"It's over," he said.

The effect was instantaneous. As one, every Keriag on the battlefield halted where it was, their black, blank eyes turned towards Fane Aracq. Even those in the path of the mighty war-machines – the few that were still operational – froze in the same manner, standing still as the immense tracks rumbled up to them and crushed them under the treads. But for these sounds, and the erratic *whumph* of the force-cannons from the palace and the wyverns flying overhead, everything went dead. The click and shuffle and clash of spear, the background sound of the battle stopped. And just for one brief moment, it was like time had frozen, and only machines and flying beasts were exempt from its grip.

A sea of alien eyes, surrounding the whole palace, all focused on one spot. The chamber of Aurin.

They exploded forward in one gargantuan concerted surge, swarming past the war-machines and spreading up the white creamstone walls like a black blight, the hooked ends of their spiderlike legs carrying them effortlessly up the sheer surface. It was as if an invisible barrier had held them back until now, physically preventing them from touching the palace; but now it had fallen, and they attacked with a vigour and savagery that was terrifying to behold. Up the walls they went, and over, scampering down into the courtyards beyond. The sound of force-cannon fire struck up anew as the Guardsmen within made a vain attempt to defend their palace, but the weight of numbers that the Keriags possessed was overwhelming. Careless of their own safety, they tore into the palace, pouring over the walls on all sides, hacking through gates, scaling walls, clambering through wind-holes. No place was safe from the Keriags; Fane Aracq had not been built to withstand such creatures as they. And as they ripped through the lower levels of the palace, their viciousness laid testament to the fact that they had been unable to purge *all* emotions from their race; for they fought with a fury that left no stone unturned, and no living being in its wake. They fought for revenge.

"Mauni's Eyes!" Hochi breathed, from where he steered the wyvern high up in the cool night sky. The spectacle, when viewed from above, was even more extraordinary. The chaotic and beautiful architecture of Fane Aracq, the asymmetry of the spikes and spires and curves, domes and blisters, was being subsumed in the squirming black of the Keriags. The sheer number of the insectile race made him feel humbled and afraid. What if the Keriags did turn on them after they were freed? What if Kia was right in her protests? Wouldn't they be an enemy with even less mercy than Macaan? Should Calica really give them back their freedom?

"He did it," Gerdi said in the harness behind him, his hands tightening where he held Hochi's belt for stability. "Whaddya know? He really *did* it!" He whooped suddenly, raising one hand in salute. "I told you he'd pull it off!"

But Calica, in the hindmost seat, couldn't smile. Somewhere down there Ryushi was still in great danger. And if he survived, then it would be her turn. To be the bearer of the heartstone. It was a responsibility that terrified her. A responsibility, of course, which depended on the plan they had formulated actually *working*.

Seeing the onslaught of the Keriags below, she wasn't sure that she even *wanted* it to work. So what if the heartstone was not fooled into thinking she was Aurin? The Keriags would die, perhaps Aurin would be killed, and Macaan's forces would be terribly weakened. Parakka's greatest threat would be eliminated, and the woman who had reportedly stolen the heart of the one who was supposed to be hers would be no more. Hardly a tragedy from her point of view.

And yet she had to try, for now her course was set. To refuse the heartstone would mean she was responsible for the genocide of an entire species. And she would never have Ryushi then, much less be able to live with herself.

But deep in a selfish part of her, she hoped and hoped that the heartstone would not accept her. Because if it did, that meant she *was* Aurin's Splitling. Aurin was what Calica could have been if things had gone a different way for her. And she did not like the suggestions that possibility made about herself.

"Let my Princess *go!*" Corm shouted, his voice high and shrill. In Ryushi's hard grip, Aurin trembled and sobbed, her composure lost with her power, a spoilt and frightened girl once more.

Ryushi loathed himself at that moment, hated himself for having to hurt a woman like this, especially *this* one. Instead, he flicked his glance over to where Tatterdemalion was getting up from the floor, cradling a broken limb across his emaciated chest.

"Don't come near," Ryushi warned the Jachyra. "I'll kill her if you do." He wondered, would he really be able to, if it came to it? Would his spirit-stones respond? Would the Damper stone stifle his power, or his own reluctance? He didn't know.

Tatterdemalion observed him hatefully, the expression somehow coming across through the metal features of the creature. **+++ The Keriags will kill us all when they arrive +++** he said, his voice more loaded with static than ever.

"Not with me here," Ryushi replied, sounding more confident than he was. He had faith that the Parakkans would have told the rampaging Keriags who they were trying to save, but he was not certain that the Keriags would recognize him. The sound of their frantic invasion was all around them.

"Ryushi, let me *go*!" Aurin sobbed. "You've got

the stone, yes? You've beaten me, you've *won*! Don't let me die, Ryushi!"

"They won't kill you," he insisted, sounding unsure now. "You'll be . . . alright with me."

"You can't keep her," Corm said, and the suddenly calm and level tone in his voice made Ryushi pay attention. He had guessed a long while ago what had been going on between the Princess and the prisoner, and he was better equipped to understand it than a Jachyra. Now it had all come to a bad end, as he knew it would. But at least he could try and save his Princess.

"I don't want—"

"Parakkan, you *do*," said Corm. "You want to keep her with you. You don't want to let her go. But you know that the rest of Kirin Taq will demand blood, even if the Keriags do not kill her first. No matter how much you want to, you cannot stop that; and even if you put your life in front of hers, retribution *will* be exacted." He paused, seeing the cold knowledge force itself on to Ryushi's face. "You must let her go, or see her die. Or give her back the heartstone. But you cannot keep her now."

"*Please*," she begged. "Let me go!"

"And where will you go?" Ryushi demanded. "To your father? What if we meet again like this, repeat this ordeal? You think I can risk that?"

"No! No, not to my father! Do you think I can face him now? Do you think I dare risk what he will *do* to me in return for losing one of his kingdoms?" She turned in his arms, and he loosed his grip so that she could, but his hand still held tight to her shoulder, ready to unleash the fatal power if either of her aides tried to attack. Now he looked into her eyes, tear-reddened but undiminished in their perfection, and she spoke low and raggedly. "You have ruined me, Ryushi. Let me go. I will leave this life you have shattered behind me, and find a new one."

"You'll not survive. Too many people know of you," Ryushi said. He was being deliberately obstructive; he could not face the choice that Corm had shown him.

"But only a few have *seen* me, and they are dying as we speak. The world knows me only by reputation, not by sight."

There was a silence in the room, but all around the sounds of conflict were getting louder with frightening rapidity. Tatterdemalion and Corm anxiously watched the two of them, their eyes burning, one with supplication, the other with indecision.

"What I did, I did because I had to," Ryushi said. "I'd made a promise, and I had to keep that promise. Because my word is my bond, even to death." He took a breath. "But you must promise me this. If I let you go, you won't return to your father. If I let you go, you are his daughter no longer, and we'll never meet again as enemies. Do you understand?"

"I understand."

"Promise me."

"I promise," she said, lowering her eyes.

"*Mean* it!"

She raised her chin, meeting his gaze defiantly. "I promise, Ryushi! I promise. My word is *my* bond, and though it has never been tested as sorely as you profess yours to have been, you will find it every bit the equal."

Ryushi searched her face, seeking deceit and finding none. Then he stepped back and let her go. She did not go immediately, just took a pace away, such a mix of emotions written on her features that he could not tell what she was feeling as she did so.

+++ My lady, we must go +++ said Tatterdemalion. Neither he nor Corm were making any move to attack. They were still wary of Ryushi's power, even without his hostage. Outside, the noise of the conflict intensified suddenly, spilling towards them.

She turned away from him, walking slowly across to the mirror. There was still a good portion of it that was not shattered, for its impregnation of powdered spirit-stone had made it tough and resilient. Corm moved with her, taking her by the elbow, leading her towards where the Jachyra waited to take them through. Aurin did not turn, did not look back as they stepped through the mirror; and then the reflective surface flowed over her like molten metal and she was gone.

The battle ended quickly after that. Their palace overrun, the Princess's Riders decided to cut their losses and save their own skins, dispersing and heading for the keeps of other nobles. Most of the palace guns had fallen silent now, their operators slaughtered by the Keriags; and so the Parakkan wyverns were left free to obliterate the few remaining war-machines, finding the slow, lumbering things easy targets for their force-cannons. The Keriags scoured the corridors of Fane Aracq, killing without mercy or remorse, until finally the killing was done.

Calica hurried along the corridor, passing between patches of light and shade from alternately whole and shattered white glowstones. She had already become numbed to the sight of blood and bodies by the time she saw the smashed remains of the sentries that had tried to bar Ryushi's way into the Princess's chambers, and the horror could not penetrate the thick hide she had developed over years of Parakkan service. Hochi and Gerdi were close by her, and surrounding them were the rapid, angular movements of the Keriags that escorted them, bringing them to where the heartstone was, bringing them to. . .

"Ryushi!" Calica cried, and rushed across the rubble-strewn room to where he stood, leaning on the windowsill, looking out of the window. She walked up next to him, placing a hand on his shoulder. "Ryushi, are you alright?" Her relief and joy at seeing him alive was tempered by his silence.

Hochi and Gerdi followed her in. All around, the Keriags stood, their spears in their hands, waiting.

Ryushi muttered something.

"What?" Calica asked, leaning closer. He repeated himself again, this time in an even more mournful cadence. "You let her *go?*" she asked in disbelief. The Keriags stirred, reflecting the discomfiture of the hive-mind. "*Why?* You idiot, *why?*" she shouted. "Didn't you think to hold on to her? Do you know what will happen now if the heartstone *doesn't* match me?"

"What do you mean?" Ryushi asked, turning his head in alarm. "You? I'm supposed to give it to *you?* And you don't even know if it will *work?*"

The Keriags shuffled more animatedly, their joints clicking, their black eyes cold and intense.

"Have you got the heartstone, Ryushi?" Hochi said, stepping forward.

In answer, Ryushi slowly held out his hand and

opened it. The silver double thread of Aurin's necklace spilled out, the three turquoise stones piled up in his palm. There was no vibration, no inner glow, no sign that it might crack and end the lives of thousands upon thousands of Keriags in a short second. The creatures around them went still.

"Put it on me," Calica said, turning around so that her back was to him. "The chain's broken. Tie it round my neck."

Ryushi hesitated a moment, then moved to comply. What if it didn't work? What if, even after everything, the Keriags died? He took a heavy breath, his eyes closing.

Father, Gerdi . . . I did my best for both of you. I tried my hardest to keep my promises. That's all I can do.

He brushed the straight fall of Calica's orange-gold hair aside, exposing her neck. He laid the heartstone against her heart, and tied the thin, double-chain of silver together behind her. He let go and stepped back.

For a time, Calica stood there, unmoving. Then she hitched in a sharp breath, suddenly, as if someone had placed something cold down her back. She closed her eyes, and kept them closed. All eyes were on her.

"Oh, for Cetra's sake, don't tell me it hasn't *worked*!" Gerdi exclaimed.

Calica's eyes flicked open, the olive of her irises misted by a sheen of saltwater. "Of course it's worked," she said, a terrible sadness in her eyes.

And all around her, the spiderlike Keriags lowered themselves until their low-slung torsos touched the creamstone floor, their spears held horizontally before them, a gesture unlike anything the others had ever seen before from the creatures. They were honouring her.

She lifted her head, her spine straight and proud, and wiped the single tear from her face. "We've won only half the battle," she said, suddenly becoming again the leader she had always been. "Takami marches on Base Usido; he may already be there. Our friends are in danger. We have to go, if we're not already too late."

"Takami?" Ryushi said. "And where is Kia?"

Calica met his gaze unflinchingly, and Ryushi felt his stomach sink.

Kia.

9

The Path of the Bolt

"Get to cover! They're firing on us!" the Dominion man shouted, running from the small metal booth at the base of the cliffs that operated the lifts, dodging through the stabbing force-bolts that rained down from above. It was only by good fortune that one of the warriors who had escaped the clifftop massacre was the Overseer of Base Usido, a tall, gaunt man with a sparse black beard named Guji; he was one of the few people privy to the self-destruct mechanisms that the Machinists had installed in most of the sensitive devices in the Base.

Peliqua and Jaan retreated a little further, to where Iriqi stood, and watched as Guji ran with great, loping strides across the scarred clearing towards them. He took shelter behind a shattered hut, one that had been torn apart by the Snagglebacks a few cycles ago and had not yet been rebuilt. A few moments later, one of the larger lifts suddenly jarred into action, the chains and pulleys clanking as it began to rise up the cliff face, summoned by the Guardsmen above in a similar booth to the one that Guji had just come from. There was a breathless pause, as the Parakkans watched the lift wheeze higher and higher . . . and then the booth imploded, folding in on itself with a thick *wham* and reducing to a heap of crushed metal. At the same time, several other mechanisms at various points up the cliff face followed suit, and the ascending lift shuddered to a halt and was still.

"That'll hold them," Guji said, his voice bubbly with phlegm. "But only till they get ropes and cables to climb down with. Get yourselves ready; we want to make their descent as painful and costly as possible."

The defenders dispersed in a flurry of activity, finding themselves what ranged weapons they could and grabbing any cover that was available. The Guardsmen on the clifftop, tiny figures at such a huge distance, fired occasional bursts of concussion down at them; but they were too far away for the bombardment to be accurate, and it was more frightening than effective. The Parakkans formed themselves into a semicircle, using the shattered huts that surrounded the clearing to hide in, and waited for the Guardsmen to try and come down.

"Peliqua! You've gotta come with me!" said a voice that suddenly piped up at her shoulder where she crouched. As one, she and her brother turned from their flimsy barricade of broken wood and looked at Elani, dust-streaked and agitated.

"Oh! What is it?" she asked, her expression mirroring the younger girl's.

"Cousin Kia's just come in through the front gate. Ty's hurt! Come on!"

It did not even occur to her that there was probably nothing she could do to help; nor did she question how Elani had known where she was – not that this was unusual for the Resonant girl, for she was an endless mine of surprises. She simply acted, getting up to go with Elani. Jaan and Iriqi went with her. Together, the four of them left the semicircle of defenders and ran across the Base, between the shattered and smoking buildings and the craters, between the living and the dead and the still-dying.

It was what saved their lives.

Anaaca's spy in Takami's court had been useful in finding out many things, but he had been unable to provide them with more than a vague indication of the amount of troops that Takami possessed, the size of the garrisons given to him when he took over the thaneship of Maar. What information the spy had been able to glean had been further muddied by the army's trip through the Rifts, where it was uncertain how many men or vehicles they had lost. So nobody expected the second fleet of wyverns to arrive until they came screaming across the Base, loosing a terrific salvo of force-bolt fire across the settlement.

Elani shrieked as she and Peliqua leaped to the floor, closely followed by Jaan, and bundled themselves into a protective heap. Iriqi did not move, but seemed to brace itself as the backlash of the explosions hit them, using its own enormous body as a shield for the others.

Splinters and divots of Kirin Taq earth blasted everywhere, dark shadows racing past them through the twilight; but in the lee of the huge creature, they were unharmed.

Jaan scrambled to his feet as the fury around them died, allowing the others to get up, their hair and eyes wild. He looked past Iriqi; and there, around the base of the cliffs, he saw that the huts they had been using for cover had been almost entirely destroyed, and the remains of those that had defended the clifftop had been destroyed with them. Anger welled up inside him, anger and helpless frustration. Such a loss of life! Even hardened as he was, he could not stop letting out a cry of pain; but nor could he deny the heady sense of relief that he had not been hiding there at the time, and he hated himself for feeling that way.

. But now something new was happening. The wyverns were landing, soaring into the Base towards the spot that their cannons had cleared; and on their backs were many more Guardsmen, a small strike force that was being brought in to attack the Parakkans from the inside.

"What's happening?" Elani wailed in distress, looking around frantically.

"Come on," Jaan said grimly. "We'd better warn Kia. She'll know what to do."

They set off again, hurrying through the newly settling debris, forcing themselves to ignore the screams and cries for aid that floated to them from near by, on the back of the ambient noise of the distant battle across the plains. In a short while, they reached the gate, where Kia was helping a dazed Ty to his feet, a pakpak standing next to them with its broad, flattish muzzle turning this way and that in alarm.

"Kia! Oh! Are you okay?" Peliqua asked, running up to her and taking Ty's other arm.

"What's going on over there?" Kia asked sharply, nodding towards the direction that they had just come from.

"We've been overrun! It's horrible, Kia! They're landing another load of Guardsmen to cover the cliff while the rest of them come down!"

"Have we got enough people to keep them out?" Kia demanded.

"I don't know! We've all been scattered!"

"How could—" Kia began, but cut herself off with a curse as she heard the first report of a Guardsman's halberd come from the cliffs, followed by another and another after it. Soon, the sounds of a new battle had begun, this one smaller and closer, as the isolated pockets of Parakkan resistance were swept up by Takami's Guardsmen, forcing them back so that the bulk of the army could abseil down the cliff face.

Kia looked around, a momentary despair gripping her. The Base had been all but levelled by the combination of the Banes' attack and then Takami's follow-up. Whatever happened now, there was little that could be salvaged from this place. Its location was known to their enemies, and nearly all their resources had been destroyed. If their companions had not managed to take Fane Aracq, then all was truly lost. But if they *had* . . . why, then there was a chance. Then they didn't *need* Base Usido any more.

Then all they had to do was survive.

"Forget the Base!" she said. "Come on! It's safer on the plains, with the others! Are there any pakpaks left in the stable-yard?"

"Pregnant females, probably," Jaan said. "Everything else would have been taken to ride."

"Go get a couple. They'll die anyway if they're left here. You'll have to risk riding them."

"What about Iriqi?" Jaan protested, indicating the enormous shape of the Koth Taraan that stood silently next to him.

((I will go now. Catch me up)) it said, the last few words clothed in warm amusement as it used the characteristically human phrase for the first time. With that, it lumbered away from them with surprising speed, its huge forearms and claws carried close to the ground as it made its way out of the gate and towards the distant battle.

"Peliqua! Get the pakpaks!" Kia said. The Kirin girl released Ty and rushed off towards the stables, hoping that they would still be standing when she got there. Near by, the sounds of the battle were getting closer. Elani chewed her dark hair nervously, having fallen quiet since the recent blast had shaken them.

"We're running *away*?" Jaan asked.

"You have a problem with that?" Kia replied, a challenge in her voice.

191

"*I* don't," he said, truthfully. He had never been one for confrontation. "But it's not at all like you."

"Look," she said. "This Base is dead and gone. If we stay here, in small groups, the Guardsmen will just wipe us out. If we go back to the plains and join the main group, we can fight out in the open. We're *winning* out there." She hefted the weight of Ty against her shoulder. "And besides, I have more than just myself to think about."

The Guardsmen were spreading out from the cliff face into the Base. He could not see them through the mess of smashed buildings and smoke, but he could hear them coming. Kia was right. If they stood here, they would fall.

They helped Ty back into the saddle, and Kia got up behind him; then Peliqua was with them again, leading two pakpaks. How she had reined them so fast he would never know, but he was glad of her efficiency. One of the beasts was heavily pregnant, its belly swelled beneath its tiny forelimbs; but the other looked like it was in the early stages, and showed no bulge at all.

"These were all I could find," she said apologetically.

"I'm lighter," Jaan said, swinging himself up on to the back of the larger one, hearing it murmur in discomfort as he got into the saddle. Peliqua mounted the other, picking Elani up with her.

"Ready?" Kia asked. "Then come on! We've got a fight to win!"

They urged their mounts forward, and the pakpaks obliged sluggishly, without any of the usual zeal of the species. Behind them, in the Base, they heard a screech and the *whoosh* of air as a number of wyverns launched themselves skyward, now that they had dropped off their cargo of troops. Bounding across the plain, their pakpak's muscular two-toed feet propelling them fast towards where Iriqi had a head start on them, Kia was suddenly conscious that they were terribly exposed out here. Between the Base and the fight that raged around the edges of the valley, there were only the dead and wounded; and there were not many of them, for they had a way to go before they reached the main battleground. She clutched harder to Ty's waist, and pushed her exhausted and overloaded pakpak onward, and sought safety in numbers.

"Cousin Kia! Up there!" Elani cried, pointing

past Peliqua's stabilizing arm and up at where the forest canopy high above them peeled back to reveal a slice of velvet sky. Seven wyverns had taken wing, soaring from the Base and passing far overhead, making for the main mass of the battle. But as Kia looked, her expression suddenly changed to concern. One of the wyverns was dropping back and peeling away from the other six, banking in a shallow downward curve, turning towards them.

"They've seen us!" she barked. "Scatter!"

The three pakpaks split up, heading away from Iriqi as the wyvern neared at frightening velocity. It was coming from directly in front of them, intending to pass low overhead, but as the Parakkans spread further and further apart its target became obvious. It was going for Kia and Ty.

Eyes narrowed against the wind of the sprinting pakpak, Kia fixed her gaze on the approaching beast, ready to gauge the moment it would strike. But her thoughts deserted her, her preparation dashed as the wyvern swooped low enough for her to see who occupied its harness. There was an Artillerist there, with a standard force-cannon on a pivot set into the pommel; but it was the sight of the rider that suddenly filled her mind.

The green, elegant, close-fitting armour. The silver mask, fashioned in the shape of a screaming spirit, its mouth distended in sorrowful agony. The long, black ponytail. Takami.

The realization stunned her enough so that the hard swerve she had intended to execute never happened. But the Artillerist had no such hesitation. He loosed a bolt over Takami's shoulder a moment before the wyvern thundered past them like a hurricane, the force of its passing blowing their pakpak to a halt and almost making it tip over backwards. And a fraction of a second later the force-bolt hit the ground a few metres away and blasted them sideways, sending beast and riders flying. Kia landed hard and awkwardly, instinct making her put out one hand to try and break her dive. There was a sickening snap as her wrist gave, and her shriek of agony was knocked from her lungs as the rest of her body hit the bloodied grass. Her leg twisted under her and cracked like a twig, and unconsciousness boiled up from behind her eyes to claim her.

Nothingness. Then –

"Cousin Kia!" Elani was shouting distantly, but everything was fogged in pain as Kia's eyes opened, and she could not respond. She could only have been out for a few seconds, but it felt like lifetimes. Ignoring the burning fire in her leg, she tried to raise herself a little, knowing that they were still in danger, not allowing her body the respite it craved. Holding her broken wrist to her chest with her other hand, she lifted her head and peered through the waxy sheen of unreality that had suddenly descended upon her.

Their pakpak lay twitching some distance away, in its final death throes. Ty was next to it, mercifully conscious but unable to move, his shirt wet with blood, his eyes searching for hers in alarm. Faintly, she was aware that the wyvern would be looping around for another strike even now, and that it carried on its back her hated brother Takami. But it was as if, suddenly, all power to act had been taken from her, as if the fall had broken more than her bones but her will also. She was an observer now, powerless, and in one terrifying, heart-twisting moment, she saw everything that was about to happen and knew that the future had locked itself on course, that there was no way to avert it.

There was a screech as the wyvern closed in for the kill, the Artillerist sighting for the blast that would finish her and Ty. She looked up dazedly, an almost bewildered expression on her face, and saw the silver mask of her brother leaning low over the neck of the wyvern, plunging towards them like the spectre of death. From somewhere behind her, she heard the thunder of pakpak feet, felt the vibration through the ground. But her eyes had turned back to meet those of her lover: sweet, sensitive Ty, Ty the Pilot's apprentice who had proved himself as good as any Master.

At least they'd die together, she thought. At least there was that.

"Cousin *Kia*!" A scream now, from the little nine-winter girl who had got them into all this in the first place.

History repeats itself, she thought, her inner voice speaking up clearly. *That's the way of war. Takami killed my father. Now he's killing Ty. It will never end.*

The Artillerist hit the firing stud. The force-cannon spat a ripple of energy, sending it racing towards where Kia and Ty lay helpless.

Peliqua's pakpak reached them at the same moment, and the Kirin girl threw herself from the saddle, carrying Elani with her. Kia was suddenly aware of them as they hit the earth, aware that they had carried themselves into the path of the bolt, aware that –

"No!" she screamed as they flung themselves on to her, the agony of her broken and grating bones nothing to the agony that stabbed through every fibre of her being as she realized what was about to happen. She reached out for Ty with her good arm, but the distance between them might as well have been a mile. Her eyes never left his as the bolt hit, and between them passed a moment of understanding too great for words, a moment of tender parting and terrible sorrow.

And then they were gone, disappearing in the heart of the shattering concussion.

"Peliquaaa!" Jaan screamed, his voice ripping and going ragged. His yellow eyes stared in denial of what he had seen, saltwater stinging

them. Takami's wyvern blasted overhead with a triumphant screech and soared away towards the battle, uninterested in the lone halfbreed boy on his pakpak or the rocklike creature that lumbered slowly back towards him.

Jaan did not turn to watch it leave. Panting, sobbing, he sat in his saddle and gazed mutely at the spot where the bolt had hit. Obliteration met his eyes. The earth had dented inwards and collapsed, opening a pit into one of the bottomless faults that zigzagged across the rifts. Dirt and blood and rubble lay everywhere, scraps of pakpak fur and unidentifiable flesh. Ty had been blown clear, face down, and Jaan did not even need to look closely to see he was dead.

But his sister, along with the Resonant girl and Kia. Of them, there was no trace. If anything remained of their bodies, it was lost to the endless depths under the earth.

He had watched his sister die.

((Jaan)) said Iriqi, and the word was so heavy with the pastel colours of sorrow and sympathy that the halfbreed boy burst into tears. The Koth Taraan stood by him for a moment as he buried his face in his hands, his thick ropes of hair falling like a curtain, the ornaments and beads in them clacking together as they shifted.

((We are sorry, Jaan. Sorry that we came too late))

The words seemed not to come from Iriqi, but from another voice: deeper, wiser and immeasurably older, and through his uncontrollable grief Jaan suddenly understood what was meant.

The Koth Taraan had arrived.

The first to be hit were the clifftop defences. Like a thunder-head the creatures had moved through the forest, slow and looming and unstoppable. In all of the Base Usido, the only one who knew of their approach was Iriqi; and he had not even mentioned it to Jaan, for the Koth Macquai wanted secrecy. Nobody had expected the attack, and it came too suddenly for the Guardsmen to react before the Koth Taraan came charging out of the treeline, gathering momentum as they came, like boulders rolling down a mountainside. Concussion-bolts thumped into them time and time again, but the halberds of the Guardsmen had little effect on the thick plates of armour that protected the creatures.

They smashed through the breach that the Guardsmen had made, hundreds upon hundreds of them, each a tower of immense strength and matchless power. Their claws went through the Guardsmen's black armour as if it were paper, and tore their bodies apart like they were held together by little more than air. The Artillerists in the force-cannon towers managed to bring their weapons to bear and began firing devastating shots off into the fray. Their more powerful weapons took the lives of several of the Koth Taraan before the enraged creatures toppled the towers and the wall with it, their combined might pushing the weakened structure outwards from the inside until it simply came apart.

It was a rampage. The Koth Taraan swatted aside Takami's Guardsmen like humans might wave off annoying insects, or clapped their huge claws together on their victims with enough force to shatter bones. They drove the terrified Guardsmen before them, pushing them to the cliff edge and over it, sending them spilling from the lip of the precipice to fall screaming to their deaths in the Base below.

In less than five Dominion minutes, it was over. Every Guardsman on the clifftop had been killed. The Koth Taraan waded in mud and gore, their wide black eyes intense as they stood in the aftermath of the slaughter. Then, silently, they moved on.

All around the cliffs, a similar scene was being played. The secret reinforcements that Takami had kept back in the trees for a final surprise found themselves set upon with terrifying savagery, by creatures with such casual strength and power that they had no defence against them. Harried mercilessly, cut down at every turn, they could only run in the face of the stampede, to be driven howling over the cruel cliffs and sent plummeting on to their comrades far below.

For Takami's forces on the plains, it was impossible to tell exactly what was going on; but they knew that something had gone terribly wrong for them. Their back ranks – those closest to the feet of the cliffs – were being crushed by the falling bodies of their comrades; and the ropes and cables that they had been using to abseil from the clifftop were being cut loose, leaving them stranded in the valley with no way back up. Until then, despite the fact that the Parakkans had been beating them on the plain, they had fought with a vigour that was borne of the knowledge that they had a trick up their sleeves. Now, with their secret reinforcements gone, they had nothing.

It started in isolated pockets, but like spots of soap in a film of oil, it spread outwards, widening circles that joined other circles until, eventually, it encompassed them all. Takami's Guardsmen were surrendering, laying down their weapons and giving themselves up. His generals knew that they were beaten, and they would not allow their men to die senselessly. All across the plain, the fighting stuttered and ceased, and the cheer of Parakka's victory spread across the winners like a ripple, rising through the twilit forest.

But for Jaan, who sat with his face still in his hands on the back of his pakpak, there was no victory at all.

10

The Wounds between the Worlds

Rain lashed the rock of the Fin Jaarek mountains, pounding at stone that had been there since the world had begun. It spattered and ran, dancing in rivulets or falling into pools whose surface jumped and splashed constantly with the excitement of new arrivals. The thin corona of the black sun of Kirin Taq was hidden behind a louring curtain of cloud, and thunder rumbled deafeningly around the peaks, humbling everything beneath its power. The sparse shivers of Glimmer plants were a muted purple, faint points of light in the darkness.

Ryushi stood in a wide gully, its uneven floor thirty feet across, banked up on three sides by hard, unforgiving rock. His back was to the roiling sky, for he was high up in the mountains. He had climbed long and hard to get here. At the end of the gully, a jagged slash of a cave mouth darkened the wet rock, many times his height. His hair hung dripping around his face, his clothes soaked, his cheeks and forehead beaded with water. The rain ran hard past his boots, plunging off the precipice behind him, inviting him to join it.

For a long time, he stood there, not feeling the rain, his blue eyes fixed on the cave mouth.

I am the last, he thought to himself. *Kia, Elani, Father, Mother, Ty. All gone. All dead. Only me left, of everything that used to be Osaka Stud. Me, and Iakami.*

Ninety cycles had passed since Fane Aracq had fallen. Ninety cycles since Jaan had told him of his twin's death. Ninety cycles since he had lost Aurin. And so much had happened in that time . . . so much, and so little of it really mattered to him any more.

For a time, he had held out hope that Kia might be alive, somehow, somewhere . . . but if she was alive, she would have returned, and as the cycles wore on he knew that he was entertaining a fool's dream. She was gone, her remains swallowed in death by the earth and soil that she had mastery over in life. Slowly, he had let his hope wither, until it had finally died completely.

The Keriags held the Ley Warrens now, the only means of transport to and from the Dominions without the use of Resonants. Those Keriags that lived in the Dominions had deserted Macaan and returned to their Warrens, where they had become an immovable force against his Guardsmen. Macaan was effectively cut off from Kirin Taq completely.

As to the forces that Aurin had commanded, they were dealt with swiftly. Aurin's nobles were deposed, for none of them had the manpower to hold out against the Keriag army. Most had been killed in Fane Aracq, as they had been gathered there for Festide; many of those who survived capitulated without a struggle. Perversely, it was the tyrannical measures that Aurin had used that made the handover of power so easy in the cities of Kirin Taq; the Keriags continued policing the land as they had always done until a suitable alternative could be found, and the Guardsmen were demobilized or turned to the use of Parakka. For the common folk, life was not vastly disrupted. The celebrations that had followed Aurin's downfall had lasted for thirty cycles, and though the new order was not without its troubles – there were riots, and uprisings over petty disputes that had festered unsettled over the years – it did not affect the daily routine of the people, and civilization went on.

And now the transition period was coming to a close, and the fledgling system of government was beginning to take root. Ryushi had no head for politics, but he knew vaguely what the leaders of Kirin Taq intended to do. Reinstate the thanes to rule over the provinces as they had before, but replace the supreme rule of King or Queen or Princess with a Council, to choose thanes and to make decisions about the welfare of the land. A Council to which anyone could be elected, rich or poor, Kirin or Dominion-born. Like the Council of Parakka.

We've won a world, he thought. For a long time, he mulled over the enormity of the statement. Parakka had liberated a land. He had been instrumental in a revolution of a scale that had not been seen since Macaan subjugated Kirin Taq, before he was born. *So why don't I care?*

So much lay unresolved behind him. Calica was still the bearer of the heartstone, carrying with her the lives of the entire Keriag species. Measures were being taken to deactivate the power of the necklace and free the Keriags once and for all, but in the interim Calica had submitted herself to the guardianship of the insectile creatures. The purpose of this was twofold: firstly, it was a sign of faith, to reassure the Keriags that they had not simply passed the reins of their civilization to a new tyrant but to one who genuinely would not use her influence to enslave them again; and secondly, because the Keriags were understandably concerned about the safety of the woman every thump of whose heart carried with it the continued survival of their race.

It was a move typical of Calica, the diplomat. She had refused the pressure from all sides to use the power of the heartstone to make the Keriags remove Macaan from the Dominions as well as Kirin Taq. That had not been part of the deal that had been made in the Ley Warren, and besides, Calica was adamant that she would not become like Aurin. Perhaps it was Calica consciously trying to distance herself from her Splitling, but more likely it had been what Ryushi had told her about the trap that the Princess had been caught in. If she made the Keriags act against their will, then she could never deactivate the stone for fear that they would kill her in reprisal; and unlike Aurin, she could not bear the responsibility of so many lives resting on her survival.

But all this meant that she, too, had been forced to leave Ryushi during his hour of need. Who was left for him? Hochi, Gerdi, Jaan and Iriqi. Perhaps he could have shared solace with Jaan's loss, but he had never been close to the halfbreed boy, and Jaan spent his time almost exclusively with Iriqi anyway. Hochi and Gerdi, then; but while they were fast friends, they were not people in whom he could confide his deepest feelings. Gerdi was too flighty and inattentive, and Hochi had his own problems, obsessed as he was with his incomplete search for the true meaning of Broken Sky and the guilt he felt at

Kia's death. He believed he had failed the memory of Banto by allowing one of his children to die, and Ryushi did not have the will to convince him otherwise, even though he did not believe it himself.

Of Takami or Aurin, there was no sign. The memory of the Princess and how he had been forced to betray her pained him anew every time he recalled it. And really, what had he gained by his betrayal? He thought of the ruin of grief that surrounded him and wondered if he had really done right in fulfilling his promise to Gerdi. After all, it could scarcely have turned out worse than it had from his point of view.

Elani. Oh, Father, I failed you. I lost the one thing I had left of you: my promise to protect her.

The only small consolation was that they had won. He smiled bitterly at the irony of the thought.

He blinked, and realized where he was again. Rain battered his face, dripping from the ends of the short, fat tentacles of his hair and plastering his clothes to his body. A booming wave of thunder broke across the mountains, the roar of the dark sky. The ache in his muscles from the chill and the long climb meant nothing to him. He savoured the physical pain, for it took his mind from the pain in his life, and made everything gloriously sharp and clear. In the ninety cycles since his sister's death he had taken to punishing his body more and more, and his lean frame was taut with muscle as a result. Perhaps he had, subconsciously, been preparing himself for this moment, for the raw exertion of the climb into the mountains to get to this cave.

There was something he had to do. He could not bear to be alone any longer.

He took a step towards the cave, and almost immediately heard the warning rumble from inside. Two bright points of amber light appeared in the darkness, cutting through the misty sheets of rain to fix on him with their pupilless glare. Something large shifted within the jagged black cave mouth.

Slowly, Ryushi reached into his shirt and drew out the Bonding-stone that hung there. He had worn it ever since he was five winters old, and it was as much a part of him as the skin of his chest.

A small, diamond-shaped stone of an unremarkable grey-white colour. He raised it to his lips and whistled, half blowing on it and half forming the note himself. Whether by chance or by fate, he hit the right pitch first time, holding a high, pure note until the stone began to tremble between his fingers. A hum surrounded him, continuing even when he drew breath to keep the constant whistle going. The amber eyes in the darkness watched him intently, transfixed.

He walked forward, his steps measured and careful, non-threatening but confident. His gaze never left that of the creature in the cave, the great bull wyvern that protected the roost. It was a big one, this. And wild bulls were particularly aggressive when defending their mate and their young. The sky-blue spirit-stones that studded Ryushi's spine were gorged with energy, ready to release it at a moment's notice if the bull should attack. But as Ryushi neared, the bull seemed to be making no move to do so; instead, it watched the Bonding-stone, entranced by its hum, under the spell of its euphoric effect.

He went into the cave, and what little light

there had been drew back as he was swallowed in the moist darkness. The pounding of the rain changed its tone as he stepped out of it, turning to a sodden rattle as it hammered on the rock all around. There was the sense of movement in front of him, the heavy click of claws on stone, the leathery rustle of wings. He did not fear. His fear was as stunted as the rest of his bushfired emotions at present. Still whistling, he reached into his belt pouch and drew out a glowstone, letting the rags that wrapped it fall free, holding it high in one hand, filling the cave with the dull orange light.

The bull that stood over him was enormous, its squat, powerful body thick with plates of bony armour. Its long neck craned towards him, the amber eyes studying him from within the protective skull-like mask of the species. It dwarfed him, huge in its power, but he stood defiant in its presence. Behind it, the cave ran further back into the mountain; and close by was the female, smaller and less bulky, its own eyes fixed on the Bonding-stone that Ryushi carried. Within the protective circle of the female's split tail, a fledgling was similarly mesmerized, its neck curled quizzically.

It was small, only the same height as Ryushi, and showed little of the shape that it would take when it was an adult. Its armour was soft, and its wings were fine and fragile and shot through with a tracery of thick veins. Its muzzle was more rounded, less defined than its parents. A bull, though; he could tell by the bone structure already. The experience of growing up on a wyvern stud had not been entirely wasted on him.

As if at an unspoken signal, the mother wyvern shifted her powerful bulk, and her twin, club-tipped tail ends curled away from her fledgling, releasing it from her protection. The fledgling looked up at its mother, squawking in bewilderment, but the mother dipped her head and gently nosed it forward, urging it towards Ryushi. For a moment, it resisted; but eventually it acquiesced, shuffling on ungainly feet across the orange-stained cave, its gaze never once leaving the Bonding-stone that was held to Ryushi's lips. The bull loomed over them as the fledgling approached the Dominion boy, close enough to touch.

This was not how the Bonding ceremony was supposed to be. Riders were Bonded to domesticated, selectively bred wyverns on a stud, with a solemn ritual accompanying the heavy responsibility that they took on. But Ryushi had no patience with ritual now; it was meaningless to him, as everything else had become meaningless. So he had climbed into the mountains, knowing that it had recently been birth-time, to seek a wild fledgling. It was part spite, part his need to be obtuse; his way of railing against the world that had let him down. He would fulfil the dream he had had ever since he was a child; but he would do it *his* way, and not by somebody else's rules. So what if he was still too young? It mattered nothing to him.

The air was charged with danger. This was no controlled ceremony. He had walked into the lair of a family of wyverns.

He stopped whistling. The hum of the stone continued for a few moments, and then tailed away to nothing. Beside him, the bull stirred its immense body at the change. The female screeched, the noise deafening in the confines of the cave. But neither made a move.

Putting down the glowstone, Ryushi took the small diamond of the Bonding-stone and held it between the fingers of both hands. It was completely smooth, and almost flat. With a sharp movement, he broke it along its edge, making two perfect diamonds of half the thickness of the stone. It came apart easily, as if his touch had suddenly polarized the two halves to repel each other. Slowly, he placed one diamond directly in the centre of his forehead. When he took his hand away, the stone stayed where it was.

He looked at the fledgling. The fledgling looked back at him with its clear amber gaze. Then, as if it had known all along what was to happen, it closed its eyes and dipped its head to him. Delicately, reverently, Ryushi positioned the stone on its forehead, between and a little above the eyes. And the link was made.

Ryushi had been told what to expect by some of the Parakkan Bonded, but words could only fall short of the experience as it hit him. The rush, the all-encompassing warmth, the giddying ecstasy of *togetherness*; the staggering complexity of assimilating the thought processes of a completely alien species; the womblike feeling of protection and support, of senseless reliance on another being for survival; and then finally, the understanding, as a level was reached, and the chain was forged.

Ryushi fell to his knees on the hard stone, sweating despite the freezing rain that had soaked his body. Panting hard, he hung his head for a moment. The link was there now, but they were not fully as one. That would take training, learning. That would come as the wyvern grew, as Ryushi grew with it. But he was Bonded. There was no going back now. It was for ever.

A smile broke out on his face, the movement of his muscles unfamiliar in his recent grief. He raised his head, and saw the fledgling looking back at him, its muzzle only inches from his nose, its breath hot on his face. Its Bonding-stone, like his, had turned from grey to a dark red.

"Your name is Araceil," he said, and it felt right. Suddenly, it all felt right. He got to his feet, a little shaken by his experience. The parent wyverns watched him closely, knowing instinctively that their fledgling was his now, and he was theirs.

Part of the family, Ryushi thought, and laughed softly.

He turned away and walked out of the cave, back into the rain, leaving the glowstone on the floor where he had put it down. The rain seemed cleansing now, its hard stripes slashing him again and again and washing him inside out. He walked to the edge of the short gully, where the cliff dropped away, and stood there for a long time, looking out over the storm-torn sky. A blaze of lightning flashed behind the peaks, and a shockwave of thunder tore across the mountains and rolled over him.

Everything was lost to him. But the game was not over yet. They had won Kirin Taq, but they had not won back their homeland. That was the true prize. Kia's deal with the Keriags had only extended as far as Kirin Taq; the insectile race were not interested in the Dominions. Gradually, the Keriags would retreat back to their Warrens, and live as they had before Macaan had come;

insular, self-sufficient, keeping to their own territory. So the Koth Macquai assured them, anyway. The truth of that remained to be seen.

Division with the eventual hope of unity, Ryushi thought. Maybe it was all part of Broken Sky. First Macaan merged Kirin Taq and the Dominions; unwittingly, he'd started it all off. Parakka could use that. An age-old hatred was beginning to heal, between the Keriags and the Koth Taraan, reunited by their shared struggle. Maybe the same was beginning to happen between the Kirins and the Dominion-folk. They'd won Kirin Taq; now they were sewing up the edges of the wounds between the worlds.

The Koth Taraan. They were the true victory. Many of them were willing to fight for Parakka, and that, at least, was something. For while Macaan massed his forces in the Dominions, Parakka would be massing their own in Kirin Taq.

Macaan. Takami, he thought, as he faced out over the dark, thunder-hammered mountains.

The real battle was yet to come.

Parakka may well have won a world,
but they paid a high price for it.
And the war still isn't over.

Can Kia *really* be dead?

There's only one way to find out. . .

Read

Broken Sky

Part Seven